THE SEARCH FOR
Belle Prater

ALSO BY RUTH WHITE

Buttermilk Hill

Tadpole

Memories of Summer

Belle Prater's Boy

Weeping Willow

Sweet Creek Holler

THE SEARCH FOR
Belle Prater

RUTH WHITE

FARRAR STRAUS GIROUX

NEW YORK

Distributed in Canada by Douglas & McIntyre Publishing Group

Printed in the United States of America

Designed by Robbin Gourley

First edition, 2005

1   3   5   7   9   10   8   6   4   2

www.fsgkidsbooks.com

Library of Congress Cataloging-in-Publication Data

White, Ruth, date.

The search for Belle Prater / Ruth White.— 1st ed.

p.   cm.

Summary: In 1955, Woodrow and his cousin Gypsy befriend a new girl in
their seventh-grade class in rural Virginia, and the three of them set off to
find Woodrow's missing mother, encountering unlikely and intriguing
coincidences along the way.

ISBN-13: 978-0-374-30853-7

ISBN-10: 0-374-30853-5

1. Abandoned children—Fiction.   2. Cousins—Fiction.   3. Family
life—Virginia—Fiction.   4. Virginia—History—20th century—Fiction.
I. Title.

PZ7.W58446 Se 2005

[Fic]—dc22

2004050600

Dedicated with affection to all those readers who wanted more

THE SEARCH FOR
Belle Prater

I ◀

My cousin, Woodrow Prater, and I, Gypsy Arbutus
Leemaster, were both seventh graders in Mr. Collins's
homeroom. We were in the same building as the high
school, and we changed classes like they did, but we
would not be considered a part of the high school until
eighth grade. That's how it was in Coal Station, Virginia,
in the fall of 1954.

Mr. Collins was a real good teacher. I'm sorry to say
he was not very good-looking, and he certainly was not
as funny as some teachers I'd had. Sometimes I didn't
even think he was very smart. I mean, I wouldn't mention it to anybody, but once on the blackboard he mis-
spelled the word *committee*. (He left off the final "e.")

Even so, everybody loved Mr. Collins. He was kind.
For example, when Cassie Caulborne joined our class in
December, he went out of his way to put her at ease.
Like Woodrow, Cassie was from the backwoods, and

she was littler than the rest of us. You could tell she was nervous about coming to a new school. So, during homeroom, Mr. Collins let her sit in the back row, where she wouldn't be so public.

Then he quietly introduced her to the class and asked her if she would like to tell us about herself. She shook her head no because I think she was too scared to speak.

"That's all right, Cassie," Mr. Collins said. "The rest of us know each other, but you don't know anybody yet, and I understand what it's like to be in a new place."

Cassie just smiled.

For our first class, English, we stayed in the same room with Mr. Collins. It was during that period that he gave us an assignment to write a page about our life. I thought this was peculiar, because we had done an oral exercise very much like this one the first week of school. Then it occurred to me that this was Mr. Collins's way of introducing Cassie and the class to each other.

During recess we socialized in our homeroom, because it was raining buckets outside. A few of us moved near Cassie to make her feel included.

"Cassie, I'll declare, with your curly red hair, you put me in mind of Little Orphan Annie," Woodrow said to her. "Did anybody ever tell you that?"

I elbowed Woodrow in the ribs because I was quite sure Cassie did not want to look like Little Orphan Annie. In the funny papers she didn't have any eyes.

"Well, she does look like her!" Woodrow said, scowling at me. Then he faced Cassie again. "Little Orphan Annie's cute and tiny like you."

Cassie blushed and smiled. After that, she was more relaxed. She even joked a bit with us.

The next day Mr. Collins asked for volunteers to read our autobiographies, as he called them, to the class. I believe he was hoping that Cassie would volunteer, and he was not disappointed. After five or six others read their papers aloud, Cassie raised her hand.

"Good," Mr. Collins said to the class. "Cassie has agreed to share the story of her life with us this morning."

Everybody turned around and looked at Cassie as she stood up. I don't know what we expected, certainly nothing extraordinary, but we were wrong.

"My full name is Cassandra Carol Caulborne," she read. "I was born twelve years ago and named after Grandma Cassandra on my mama's side. She was born with a caul, and so was I.

"My mama died when I was born, so Gram was the closest thing I had to a mother, and after she died, too, I had no one but Pap, who is a quiet, good man. He has huge hands and broad shoulders. He really loves me and shows it in many ways. Because of him and Gram, I never missed my mother as much as I might have.

"On our own, me and Pap lived up Caulborne Holler,

which was named after my ancestors, and was once crawling with them, but now my kin are scattered all over these hills, and I was the last true Caulborne living in Caulborne Holler.

"A month ago our old pickup truck finally died on us. That's when me and Pap decided to move to Coal Station so that Pap could be close enough to walk to the bus station, where he is a driver.

"We moved into a house across the river by the railroad tracks. From our front porch we can see the backs of the business buildings in Coal Station. Even though our house is small and on the wrong side of the tracks, I like it.

"In Caulborne Holler I attended John L. Lewis Elementary School. By the time I got to the seventh grade, I was a big fish in a little pond, but now at Coal Station I am a little fish in a big pond. Still, I know I am going to like it here. I have always liked school.

"I love reading history better than anything. That's because sometimes I get so caught up in it, I think I am there. And when I gaze upon certain pictures from the distant past, I have feelings of homesickness."

Cassie finished abruptly, and sat down. Immediately Woodrow raised his hand and waved it around frantically.

"Yes, Woodrow," Mr. Collins said.

"What does it mean to be born with a caul?" Woodrow said.

"Cassie?" Mr. Collins said, directing the question to her, because he had no more idea than Woodrow did.

"Don't y'all know about the Caulbornes?" Cassie said. We all shook our heads no.

"Well . . ." Cassie hesitated. She had no script in front of her now, and she had to find the right words with all those eyes watching her. "Well . . . you see, the Caulbornes helped settle these mountains more'n a hundred years ago. They come over from the homeland of Ireland where they were not treated good 'cause they had the gift. Over there folks made them out to be witches and devils."

"What is the gift?" Flo Muncy asked.

"The gift of knowing without hearing or seeing. It's the second sight."

"Oh, I've heard of that," I blurted out. "It's the sixth sense—knowing things without the use of the five known senses."

"That's it," Cassie said, then smiled at me, and went on with more confidence. "In Ireland the Caulbornes had an ordinary name—Mc-Something—but when they came over here, they made up a whole new name which to this day we're proud to own, and it tells the world what we are."

"Exactly what are you?" Woodrow said.

Cassie no longer hesitated. "One of us is born with a caul every second generation. This time it's me. Next time it will be one of my grandchildren."

"But what is a caul?" Franklin Delano asked.

"It's a thick veil that covers the baby's face when it's born. That's how everybody knows you have the gift. When you're born with a caul, you know things all your life without seeing or being told."

Woodrow and I exchanged significant glances. Yeah, Cassie Caulborne was our kind of person.

"If you was in a poker game," Buzz Osborne said to Cassie, "could you tell when an ace was coming up?"

"No," Cassie said. "It don't work that way. My gram always reminded me that I am not in charge of the gift. It's in charge of me, and I don't always know when it's gonna open a door for me."

"If the gift came from your mother's side of the family, how is it that you have the name of Caulborne?" Mr. Collins wanted to know.

"Because whoever marries a Caulborne woman has to agree to take her name, so as to keep it and the legacy alive. That's how Pap became a Caulborne when he married my mother."

"So when you marry," Woodrow said, "your husband will become Mr. Cassie Caulborne?"

Everybody laughed, including Cassie.

"No, just the last name," she said.

"I must say, I find this fascinating," Mr. Collins said. "And tell me, Cassie, why are you a year younger than your classmates?"

"Oh, that's because I could already read when I started school, so they moved me right on up a grade."

"And who taught you to read, my dear?"

Only Mr. Collins would ever say a thing like "my dear."

"Why, nobody taught me, Mr. Collins. I just knew. I reckon I *always* knew. The same as I know how to take fire out of a burn. And how to stop the flow of blood from a wound. It's just something I know."

The class was puzzled, but respectful, and Cassie was glowing. She had made a good impression her second day in a new school. After that, it was like she had always been with us.

2 ◄

A few weeks later, on New Year's Eve, we were celebrating Woodrow's thirteenth birthday next door at
Granny and Grandpa Ball's house. Seated around the big
wooden table with them were my mama, Love Ball Dotson; my stepfather, Porter Dotson, owner and editor of
the local newspaper, the *Mountain Echo*; Porter's brother,
Dr. Hubert Dotson, affectionately known as Doc Dot; his
wife, Irene; their twin girls, Dottie and DeeDee, who
were four years old; and, of course, me and Woodrow.

By this time Woodrow had been living in Coal Station
for eight months. Before then he had always lived up in
an isolated holler called Crooked Ridge. He had moved
in with Granny and Grandpa when his daddy started
drinking too much, following the disappearance of his
wife and Woodrow's mother, Belle Ball Prater. That
event had been so mysterious, and so traumatic to our
family, that she was never far from our thoughts.

Any time you got Porter, Doc Dot, and Grandpa together, you could be sure there would be a little blackberry wine and a lot of very loud joking around, because
Grandpa and Granny were both hard of hearing. Doc
Dot started the fun during dinner by shouting a story
about one of his patients who came into his office with a
banana in one ear, a cucumber in the other, and a carrot
sticking up each nostril.

"Doc, I don't feel so good," the man said. "Whatsa
matter with me?"

And Doc said, "It's obvious, my man, you don't eat
right!"

When we had all finished laughing, Woodrow said,
"Now, Gypsy, you tell one."

"I thought you'd never ask," I said.

Joke telling and piano playing were my two specialties.
Everybody said so. I proceeded to tell a joke I had been
saving up for an occasion such as this.

"These three mama potatoes all got together, see, and
they started into bragging about their daughters," I said.

"And the first mama said, 'My daughter is gonna
marry a royal Irish tater!'

"And the other mamas went 'Ooo' and 'Ahh.'

"And the second mama said, 'Well, that's nothing. My
daughter is gonna marry a rich sweet tater!'

"And the other mamas went 'Ooo' and 'Ahh.'

"Then the third mama said, 'Well, *my* daughter's

gonna marry the television newsman John Cameron Swayze!'

"'John Cameron Swayze!' The other mamas sneered at her and laughed and said, 'Why, he ain't nothing but a commentator!'"

While everybody was laughing at my joke, Grandpa's German shepherd, Dawg, nudged me from under the table, and I slipped a piece of turkey to her. She had been creeping back and forth between me and Woodrow to gobble up our scraps.

Granny, Mama, and Irene had been cooking all day, so we were blessed with not only turkey and the fixins but also ham, salads, four kinds of vegetables, hot rolls with real butter, and sweet iced tea. Grandpa said some people don't see this much food in a month.

And Porter said, "Well, I, for one, won't have to eat again for a month."

"Just listen to him," Mama teased. "He'll be eating again before he goes to bed tonight."

Porter smiled at Mama and touched her hand where it rested beside her tea glass. There was a time when they would not have been comfortable doing that in front of me, because I had been what you might call hostile toward my stepfather. But Lordy, you can get tired of being mad all the time.

At the end of the meal, Granny brought out a birthday cake with thirteen candles for Woodrow, and he blew them all out in one breath, while we sang "Happy Birthday" to him. Then there were presents for him to open, and his face became so flushed with excitement, you hardly noticed that behind his thick glasses, Woodrow had crossed eyes.

Shortly before midnight we gathered in front of the TV to watch the ball drop in Times Square. Grandpa puffed up when everybody commented on how much improved his television reception was. Just a while back, you could hardly make out people's faces on the only channel available, especially if the weather was bad, but now there were two channels coming in, with hardly any interference ever.

The cause of this improvement came about right before Christmas when a bunch of fellows in town, led by Grandpa, had constructed a homemade antenna from bed rails and erected it on the top of the mountain. They christened it the Christmas Tower. Everybody who owned a television set in Coal Station had strung their TV lines up the mountain and hooked on to it. Now Mama and Porter were talking about buying a TV set for us.

When Grandpa stood in the middle of the living room floor to make an announcement, we turned the volume down.

"It's time for our New Year's Revelations," he said. "It's an annual tradition in our house. Now, if you want to know the difference between a New Year's Revelation and a New Year's Resolution, then lend an ear, for I am about to tell you."

Grandpa got awful wordy when he drank blackberry wine.

"A revelation is a disclosure, something you are revealing for the first time. And in our family, it's something you want to get off your chest. It started when me and Granny were celebrating our first New Year's Eve together after we got married. That was the evening she told me that it drove her crazy the way I sucked my teeth after dinner, and—"

"Do what!" Woodrow exclaimed.

"Yeah," Grandpa said. "Don't you know what teeth sucking is?"

Woodrow shook his head.

"Then I'll show you," Grandpa said, and screwed his mouth up funny.

"Please don't!" Granny said.

But it was too late. Grandpa was standing there in the middle of the living room, making a clacking sound with his tongue against his teeth.

"Anyway," Grandpa said, when the laughter had settled down, "that was the year we started our New Year's Revelations. When Love and Belle got old enough to join in, they started doing it, too. Every year on New Year's Eve we tell something that bothers us. You can revelate to just one person if you want to, or you can do it openly in front of everybody.

"I remember one year when Belle was about thirteen. She'd been holding it in for most of the year, but she saw this as her chance. Once she got started, she had a pure tee fit."

"'Bout whut?" Woodrow said.

"I remember," Granny said. "It was about how we made fun of her hopes and dreams. She was always talking about flying, you know. When she was little, she wanted to be Peter Pan or the angel in the Christmas play."

"And don't forget the grapevine swinging on the hillside," Mama reminded her.

"Oh, yeah, the grapevine swinging. She wanted to be Tarzan, too," Granny said.

We all laughed softly.

"Then when she was older," Grandpa continued the story, "she wanted to strap on a parachute and jump out of an airplane. By the time Belle made her revelation, she was gettin' serious. She wanted to be an airplane pilot. Nothin' else would do."

"But, you know, at this point in her life," Granny said, "we'd heard so much about this flying business that we didn't pay attention to her anymore. We'd just laugh whenever she said something about it. And that's what burned her up—the way the rest of us brushed her off."

"She complained that we had taught her to believe in her dreams," Grandpa said, "but that when she tried to tell us what her dreams were, we all laughed at her. She had a legitimate complaint."

"Yeah, she did," Granny agreed. "And we never realized before how much flying meant to her, and how much our laughter disturbed her. But she sure let us have it. And we tried to do better after that."

"Funny thing, though," Grandpa said. "We didn't hear much about flying anymore. It was almost like once she had us on her side, she got bored with it."

Woodrow was hanging on to every word about his mother. "She still talked about it once in a while," he said, "but not a lot. She dreamed about flying out of Crooked Ridge over the mountains."

Everyone was quiet for a moment. With sad, affectionate smiles, we were each lost in private thoughts of Belle.

"Anyway," Granny finally said, "the New Year's Revelation does help to clear the air. You have a whole year to think about what you're going to reveal so's you don't say something frivolous."

"Yeah," I said, "tooth sucking is pretty important stuff."

"When you hear what bugs somebody else, it makes you more considerate," Granny said.

"I got one!" Woodrow blurted out.

"Don't you want to think about it first?" Grandpa said. "You only get one revelation a year."

"No," he said emphatically. "The thing I want to get off my chest is about my daddy. I know he's not here to listen to my revelation, but that's the very thing I'm sick and tired of! He never comes to see me or call me anymore. He didn't even come at Christmas."

Woodrow paused and looked around at the sympathetic faces.

"I sent him a card on his birthday and at Christmas, and a Christmas present that Granny made with her own two hands, and do you think he even told me boo? No! Sometimes I feel like he's disappeared, too."

I couldn't have said all of that without crying, but Woodrow wasn't feeling sorry for himself. He was just mad.

"Yeah!" I said, trying to support Woodrow. "It's enough to make you wanna throw your hands up and say to heck with him!"

"Right!" Woodrow agreed. "That's what I want to do. He was never really good to me and Mama anyhow."

At those words my mama, Granny, and Grandpa stiffened and stared at Woodrow with stricken faces.

"He didn't act like he loved her," Woodrow continued. "When he drank liquor, he neglected her—and me too."

"How did he neglect y'all?" Grandpa said softly as he eased down on a chair.

"He didn't do things for us that a daddy should do. He just thought about his own self."

"Did you have enough to eat?" Mama said in a whisper.

"Most of the time, but—"

Woodrow stopped short, seeming suddenly self-conscious with all eyes on him. During his months with us he had talked sparingly about what kind of life he and Aunt Belle had lived. And I don't think he meant to say all of that.

"Anyway, that's my revelation," he said with a shrug, and abruptly turned to me. "What's yours, Gypsy?"

Before I could answer, Irene squealed, "The ball is about to drop!" Then she made three quick steps across the floor and turned the volume up on the TV.

"Five . . . four . . . three . . . two . . . *one!*"

"Happy New Year!"

A great cheer went up from the people in Times Square, and also from us. Dottie and DeeDee began blowing their noisemakers, and Dawg jumped around and barked. At the same time I heard a ringing sound. I didn't realize right then that it was the telephone. For the next few moments I was busy hugging everybody and yelling, "Happy New Year!"

Then I became aware of Porter trying to shush us because he couldn't hear what was being said on the phone. We all got quiet and Mama turned the TV down again.

"Hello! Hello! Who's there?"

Porter waited for a moment, then said, "Hello, this is the Ball residence."

Porter clutched the receiver tight against his ear.

"Who's calling, please?"

Then he listened some more.

Woodrow had gone over to stand beside Porter. As he rested the phone back in its cradle, Porter looked down at Woodrow.

"It was her, wadn't it?" Woodrow whispered.

Her who?

"I don't know, son," Porter said. "I heard only breathing, then whoever it was hung up."

"I know it was her," Woodrow said calmly. "The phone rang right on the stroke of midnight. That's the moment I was born thirteen years ago. It was her way of wishing me a happy birthday."

The room was so quiet then that you could hear the sound of fireworks from the direction of Main Street. Could it really have been Aunt Belle calling Woodrow at that special moment they had always shared?

"How would she know you are here?" Granny said.

"She knew you would take me in. She knows. I'm sure of it."

"Call the operator!" Mama said. "Find out where the call came from."

"Good idea," Porter said, and did as Mama suggested.

In a few moments he was giving the necessary information to the operator.

Then he said, "Thank you," and hung up.

He turned to look at all of our expectant faces. His own face was sober.

"It came from a pay phone in Bluefield," he said.

Bluefield was a medium-sized town sixty miles east of us right on the Virginia/West Virginia state line.

"Then that's where she is," Woodrow said.

Woodrow wanted us to go look for his mama right then and there, but the grown-ups said it would be like looking for a needle in a haystack.

"Believe me," Grandpa said, "if I thought there was any hope of finding her, we'd go."

But Woodrow and I couldn't let it be. A few days later the two of us were walking home from school, discussing the seemingly remote possibility of going to Bluefield on the bus by ourselves to look for Aunt Belle.

"But, Gypsy, your mama will never let you go," Woodrow said.

"Right! And I know Grandpa and Granny will jump at the chance to let you go without a grown-up," I said sarcastically.

"No," he admitted, "but I think my chances with them are better than yours are with Aunt Love."

"What about Porter?" I asked. "He's the only one of the four who doesn't think we still need a babysitter."

"That's it!" Woodrow said. "We should go to Porter first."

Half an hour later we were walking into my stepfather's office at the *Mountain Echo* building down on Main Street. His work space was just a cubbyhole really, partitioned off with a glass wall from the rest of the large press room. Through the glass we could see that Porter was busy on the phone, but he motioned us to come in and sit down across from his desk.

Porter was jotting down notes on a pad. It was obvious he was taking a story from somebody over the phone, which could take a while, so I looked around at the pictures displayed on his wall. There was one of Main Street in 1933; another of the championship Coal Station High School football team in 1949; and of course, Porter and Doc Dot's father, who started the newspaper in 1925. On Porter's desk was a gold-framed portrait of Mama, looking as beautiful as a movie star, and beside it, to my surprise, was a picture of me. The last time I was in this office, it had not been there, and I was pleased to see it.

I always did like the atmosphere of the newspaper office. It hummed busily, and I could smell the printer's ink on fresh news pages rolling off the press. Maybe I could get a job here when I was older.

"All right," Porter was saying to the person on the phone. "See what you can find out about the school board meeting. Talk to you later."

He hung up the phone, stuck his pencil behind one ear, and looked at me and Woodrow. "To what do I owe the honor of this rare visit?"

"Nothing special," Woodrow said. "Just wanted to see you, that's all."

Porter laughed. "Try again, Woodrow. What are y'all up to now?"

Woodrow grinned. "Yeah, you're right."

Then he told Porter what we were up to.

"Woodrow wants to look for his mama," I said after Woodrow's explanation, "and I want to help him. But you know how *my* mama is. She acts like I'm still in diapers, and Granny and Grandpa are not much better."

"Yeah," Woodrow added.

Porter listened, then he looked at us as he played around with a paper clip. You could tell he was thinking.

"So what do you want me to do?" he said at last. "I don't usually interfere when it comes to your upbringing."

"A little interference never hurt anybody," Woodrow said.

Porter laughed again, and said, "It's funny you should bring this up now. I was just thinking a while ago about Belle's New Year's Revelation when she was your age.

She actually managed to change certain attitudes of those around her. Don't you think that's quite a feat for a thirteen-year-old?"

Soon it was quitting time at the paper, and we found ourselves walking home with Porter. The three of us had developed a plan.

That evening we had dinner at Granny's table, as we often did during a school week. Mama, who was the speech and drama teacher at the high school, appreciated the break from cooking, and Granny loved to feed people.

For the greater part of the meal we held our routine high-volume conversations. We talked about the Christmas Tower and the new RCA Victor television set Mama had picked out for us at the furniture store. It was only a floor model. Our actual set had to be ordered from Bristol and would probably arrive next week.

Woodrow and I were asked about school, and how we were doing in Mr. Yates's math class, where both of us had made less than satisfactory marks last grading period. They asked about little Cassie Caulborne, and if she was fitting in at school all right.

When Mama started a funny story about something that happened in one of her classes, Woodrow glanced at his new watch, which had been a Christmas present, then caught Porter's eye.

As soon as Mama finished speaking, Porter spoke up. "By the way, we got so excited about that phone call on

New Year's Eve, we never did get to make our New Year's Revelations."

"That's right," Mama said. "Do you have something you want to get off your chest?"

"No, I'm fine. I thought maybe somebody else might have a bone to pick, and didn't get a chance that night."

"I said my bit," Woodrow said. "What about you, Granny? Or Grandpa?"

They shook their heads no.

"Aunt Love?" Woodrow said.

"Not this year," Love said.

"Well, I guess we're a happy bunch, then," Porter said. "No problems in this family."

That was my cue.

"That's right, never mind asking *me* anything," I said. "After all, I'm only the baby."

Mama, Granny, and Grandpa all stopped eating and looked at me.

"I'm sorry, Gypsy" was Porter's next line. "I just assumed . . ."

"Assumed what? That the baby can't possibly have any complaints?"

They all went silent, waiting and watching me expectantly. I pushed peas around on my plate.

"That's how I get treated around here," I said.

Mama had such a funny expression on her face, I almost laughed.

"Well, go on," she said. "Now's your chance. Tell it all."

"I have done only one really naughty thing in my whole life, and that was to chop all my hair off," I said. "Yet y'all act like I can't be trusted . . . or something."

I paused, and Mama said, "It's true, honey. You have always been well behaved."

"Then why am I treated like a baby?"

"For example?" Mama said.

"For one thing, you still pick out my clothes for me when we go shopping. For another, when I go to see Doc Dot you won't even let me go into his office by myself. And . . . and . . ."

I forgot what else I was supposed to say, so I cut to the chase.

"And the worst part is that I am never allowed to go *anywhere* without you or Porter or Granny or Grandpa."

"Where do you want to go?" Mama said.

I hadn't expected to answer this question so soon. I looked to Porter for help, but it was Woodrow who bailed me out.

"I have noticed that myself," he said. "For one thing, y'all won't let me and Gypsy go to the show at night by ourselves, when the movie theater is just right down there on Main Street, no more than a five-minute walk."

Mama's and Granny's eyes met.

"You think the dark's gonna swallow us up between there and here?" he went on.

"Well . . ." Mama said.

"We can always reconsider," Granny spoke up.

"Mama, do you realize I have never been outside of Coal Station without you?" I said.

Mama was silent.

"You know, if I join the high school band next year like you want me to, I will be going to all kinds of places without you."

"Does that worry you, Gypsy?"

"No, that does not worry me! But I think it worries you, and you need to turn me loose now, so I can get a bit of practice in walking out into the world by myself."

Porter had contributed those words. I thought they sounded rather eloquent.

"Is that all?" Mama said.

"No, I had planned to say more, but I can't think of the rest right now," I said.

"So you have been thinking about this for some time?" Mama said.

"Yeah."

"You have given me food for thought," she admitted. "And I thank you for speaking your mind."

The remainder of the meal was eaten in near silence, as we let Mama digest my revelation.

4 ◄

That's how it happened that, after much discussion, Mama, Granny, and Grandpa reluctantly agreed to allow me and Woodrow to go to Bluefield, West Virginia, on the bus by ourselves. It was Porter who finally convinced them that he would like to know what was wrong with two nearly grown youngsters going a mere sixty miles on a bus by themselves. Could they answer him that, for Pete's sake? He, for one, was sick and tired of hearing about it. Belle Prater, after all, was Woodrow's mother, and he thought if the boy wanted to go and look for her, no matter how unlikely it was that he would find her, then he should be allowed to do it.

"But how is he going to do that?" Granny wanted to know. "Woodrow knows nothing about Bluefield."

"So what? It's not that big a place," Porter said.

And finally we had won. We were granted permission to go and ask around down there, and show Aunt Belle's picture, but we had to promise to watch the time so we would not miss the evening bus home.

We had learned from our recess conversations with Cassie Caulborne that her daddy drove the Bluefield bus route, and that on nonschool days she rode shotgun for him. She was clearly surprised the following Saturday morning when Woodrow and I climbed onto the bus. In fact, she seemed a bit flustered, probably because this was a whole different part of her life from school and she found it odd to mix these two worlds. She introduced us to her daddy, and told us we could call him Pap like everybody else did. She said she helped him by collecting the money and talking to the passengers, which was a thing she was pretty good at and he was not. In fact, she had told us that Pap was no talker at all and did it only when he had to.

On that day the bus was half full of coal miners' wives with their weary eyes and chapped hands; hillbillies in overalls, with their roll-your-own cigarettes stuck into their hatbands; and an assortment of other folks, all heading out of Coal Station for various reasons, on the Black and White Transit. Some of them were regulars. They greeted Cassie by name and addressed her daddy as Pap just like she did.

Woodrow and I were so excited we could barely wait for the bus to leave the depot, but Pap seemed to be in no big hurry. He had started the engine and turned on the heat. Now he let the bus idle as he waited for last-minute passengers.

I removed my new navy coat, which had been a Christmas gift from Mama, and placed it carefully in the wire rack that ran the length of the bus. Underneath, I was wearing a bright pink sweater and wool pants that had a streak of that same color of pink running through the gray. I tossed my head and ran my fingers through my blond hair to fluff it up some.

Settling into the front seat by the door with Woodrow, I felt my face burn when he whispered to me that I looked like a pink flamingo among pigeons. I guess he meant it as a compliment, but that day I didn't want to be a pink flamingo! I just wanted to be a pigeon.

Cassie was on the seat across the aisle from us, behind Pap, and I stole a look at her clothes. She was wearing an old pair of brown corduroy slacks and a tan sweater with fuzzies all over the front, like it had been washed too many times.

Why hadn't I had the sense to wear jeans? Woodrow had his on. Why hadn't he reminded me that this was not a fashion show we were going to? I was so used to trying to please Mama that I didn't even think for myself. I just automatically reached for the most stylish thing in my closet.

Finally the bus left the depot and lurched up Main

Street to the one stoplight, which was green, and we headed out Route 460 as it curled through the mountains following the river.

Cassie announced to the passengers, "First stop is Lucky Ridge! We'll be loadin' and unloadin' folks, and we'll be there for maybe fifteen minutes; so if nature calls, you can go, or if you want some nickel food, they got pop and stuff in Joe's Grocery."

An old toothless man in the seat behind us tapped Woodrow on the head and said, "You young'uns got business in Bluefield today?"

"Just going to look around," Woodrow said, glancing back at the man. "I never been there before."

The man cackled. "You ain't missed nothing. You coming home on the evening bus?"

"Yeah," Woodrow said.

"Well, you be careful you don't get lost while you're looking around. Take my advice and read the street signs. I'd shore hate for you to miss the bus home. Bluefield ain't like Coal Station with just one street to it. There's maybe ten or 'leven streets in Bluefield, and they all look alike to me."

Woodrow nodded politely and turned his face frontward, but the man didn't let up. He tapped Woodrow's head again.

"I'm going to see my sister, Tulip," the man went on.

"She's been living in Bluefield since 1942, and I go to see her about once't or twice't a year. But it took me a long time to learn how to git to her house and back to the bus station. I finally figgered out I orta read the street signs. So you make sure to read the signs."

That's when I got tickled. I couldn't help it.

Cassie, in an effort to peel the toothless man off Woodrow's back, suddenly yelled from across the aisle, "Woodrow! Have you ever heard of Lady Jane Grey?"

I happened to know that Lady Jane Grey was one of the queens of England centuries ago.

"Na . . . aww," Woodrow said slowly, shaking his head from side to side. "Don't think so. She live around here?"

Cassie and I both laughed at that one.

"Lady Jane Grey was a sixteen-year-old girl a long, long time ago," Cassie said, "who was on the throne of England for only nine days. That's why she was called the Nine-Day Queen. I have read four books about her."

"'Zat so?" Woodrow said. "Well, history's not my best subject. In fact, I've been in trouble more than once over a history lesson."

"How's that?" Cassie said.

"Well," said Woodrow, "one day my teacher, Miz McIntosh, said I was being a smart aleck, but I was just trying to answer her question. She asked the class where was the Declaration of Independence signed, see? And I said at the bottom, I reckon, and—"

Cassie hooted. "You did not!"

"Yeah, I did," he said innocently. "Wadn't that a good answer?"

Before she could respond, Woodrow leapt into another story. He was on a roll. "Another time we were talking about the presidents, and Miz McIntosh sez in her sweet schoolteacher voice, 'Boys and girls, what do you reckon Thomas Jefferson would say if he were alive today?'

"And I sez, 'He'd prob'ly holler, 'Somebody let me out of this grave!'"

I laughed along with Cassie though I had heard the joke before. In the short time Cassie had been in our school, she had not yet seen this mischievous and lighthearted side of my cousin. I could tell she was charmed.

A few minutes later the repetitious old codger tapped Woodrow on the head again and said, "Hey, sonny, it's Graham Street that runs past the bus station. Remember to read the signs!"

And that was only the first ten minutes of our trip.

5 ◄

We had started snaking around and around and up the mountain toward Lucky Ridge when a massive red-faced woman lit up a pipe. I clutched my tummy.

"I guess you're not used to these smells on the bus," Cassie said. "And the hairpin curves. It's been a long time since I had motion sickness, but I remember how it feels. It's awful."

Then a baby, maybe two months old, started squalling.

"Reckon we'll have to listen to that all the way to Bluefield?" Woodrow asked.

"That's June Honaker's new baby," Cassie said. "She'll stick something in its mouth drek'ly."

I looked out at the sky, which was a perfect blue with only a few fluffy white clouds in it. Even though the sun was shining bright, Pap had the heater running wide open because it was cold and windy out there. This was my least favorite time of the year to look at the trees, because they were so skinny and brown. You could see the cliffs and the slate dumps, and strip mines all up and down the sides of the hills, which you couldn't see that good when the leaves were full and green.

The bus took a sharp curve, and my tummy rolled.

"Gypsy's turning green," Woodrow said to Cassie.

Timidly she looked back to where the pipe smoker was. "I don't know her," she whispered. "She's awful big."

About that time the woman opened her window and knocked the fire from her pipe out of it. At the same time, the baby hushed. My stomach settled. It was a miracle. The bus was quiet then, except for somebody snoring, and I was able to put my mind on other things.

Woodrow stood up and leaned over me to look at the steep drop-off on our side of the road. It was a long way down.

"If Pap should move that wheel just a wee bit too much to the right we'd drop like a rock to the bottom of the mountain," he said. "We'd be goners for sure."

"Pap is the best driver in the world," Cassie said. "And there's no cause for worry."

Ever since meeting Cassie, Woodrow and I had talked about her gift, and wondered if she could help in finding out where Aunt Belle was. Now, I guess, Woodrow figured the time seemed right to bring up the subject.

"Cassie, you say you got the gift?" he said.

"Yeah, I do."

"Then maybe you can tell me something important."

"Where your mama is?" Cassie said.

"Joe Palooka! How did you know what I was going to say?" Woodrow said with awe in his voice, like he was real impressed.

"Everybody knows about Belle Prater disappearing," Cassie said. "Me and Pap read about it in the *Mountain Echo* when it happened, and I focused on her picture, hoping maybe I would get a clue, but nothing came to me. The kids in our class told me you were Belle Prater's boy."

Woodrow told Cassie about the New Year's Eve phone call.

"So we decided to go to Bluefield and have a look-see," Woodrow went on.

"How come your grandpa didn't bring you?" Cassie asked.

"He didn't think we could find her," I said.

"That's right," Woodrow said. "Besides, we wanted to do this by ourselves."

The road became more and more winding as we reached the top of the mountain. Far down in the bottom of the holler you could see a coal camp with all its brown look-alike houses lined up against the base of the mountain. There was a littered dirt road running in front of the row. You could see frozen overalls hanging on a clothesline, and outdoor toilets and water pumps between the houses, because they didn't have indoor plumbing. It was like looking down into a big trashy hole, but people actually lived there.

"We're coming up on Lucky Ridge," Cassie said. "We'll go into Joe's and set down for a few minutes where it's warm, so we can talk."

Shortly we were pulling up in front of a country store at the top of the world. You could see nearabout a hundred miles in every direction. As we got off the bus, we saw five or six people waiting to board, three of them little kids.

"Oh no!" Cassie said when she saw them. "There's them Lucky young'uns. They'll aggravate the tar out of us. Don't give 'em a lick of attention, you heah? Not one lick. Or they won't leave us alone."

The wind was whipping around us and whistling through the shivering trees, so that we pulled our coats tight and hurried into Joe's Grocery, where we sat on a bench beside a potbellied coal stove and warmed ourselves.

"Cassie, do you know your way around Bluefield?" Woodrow said.

"Yeah," Cassie said. "Sometimes I shop there while Pap does his run to Johnson City. I usually have time to kill, so I go to the library and read a book, or I go to the dime store and buy a comic book. Sometimes I hang around one of the drugstores and have a fountain Coke and play the jukebox. One time I went to a show. I've learned the streets pretty good."

"Do you think Pap will let you go with us today?" Woodrow asked hopefully.

"Shore he will!" Cassie said quickly, happily.

Woodrow reached into his shirt pocket, pulled out a photo of Aunt Belle, and handed it to Cassie.

"This is her," he said softly.

It showed an ordinary-looking woman with brown hair and nice eyes.

"She was peculiar, I reckon, to most folks' way of thinking," Woodrow said as he took the picture back and gazed at it fondly. "I understood her, but I don't think anybody else did. She liked things we would like. You know, kid things—comic books and ghost stories and magic. And her piano playing was so sweet, it made you wanna cry. Sometimes I can feel her near me."

"What do you mean?" Cassie said.

"Do you remember the day after Christmas when it started snowing late in the afternoon?" Woodrow said as he placed the photo carefully back into his shirt pocket.

Cassie nodded. Woodrow had already told me this story on the day it happened, but I was glad to hear it again.

"Well, I was in my room, laying on my bed reading, when all of a sudden Mama popped into my head. So I put down my book and thought about her. The room was dim and cool, and I knew the snow clouds were gathering above. I felt bad 'cause me and Mama had always enjoyed playing in the snow together.

"I could hear sounds from downstairs, and I was thinking how comfortable it is living with Granny and Grandpa, and I know they love me. Life is a whole lot easier now than it ever was with Mama and Daddy on Crooked Ridge. So why couldn't I let her go?

"A stillness came, and I opened my eyes just a sliver. The room had turned a silver blue, and there was the faintest scent of mountain laurel, which was a favorite smell of Mama's. The air seemed to move like there was a breeze blowing through, but all the windows were shut tight.

"I had a funny sensation then right beside my ear, and I heard her voice just as clear and sweet.

"'Oh, look, Woodrow! Look!' she said. 'It's snowing.'

"I whispered, 'Mama!' and I jerked myself straight up in bed.

"But of course she was nowhere to be seen. I went to the window and saw that snow was falling on the orchard.

"I said, 'Yeah, Mama, it's snowing here, too,' and I know she heard me."

Woodrow fell silent.

"That is fey," Cassie said in a whisper. "You smelled the mountain laurel, you heard her voice; then when you went to the window you saw it was snowing."

"That's right," Woodrow said, also whispering. "It was like she was there telling me to go to the window and see the snow, like she used to do."

"What do you mean by *fey*?" I leaned over and joined in the whispering.

"It means magical, and beyond the natural way of things," Cassie said. "Woodrow's mama was talking to him from afar. That happens to people who are real real close to each other in here."

And Cassie touched her heart tenderly.

6 ◀

When we reboarded the bus, Cassie asked Pap if she could go with me and Woodrow in Bluefield. Pap said he reckoned so, as long as we were at the bus station at five o'clock when he returned from Johnson City.

Cassie squeezed into the same seat with me and Woodrow so we wouldn't have to talk across the aisle. I was at the window, Woodrow was in the middle, and Cassie was on the aisle side so she could jump up in a hurry to help Pap if she had to.

The toothless man had moved to the last seat of the bus, where he was blissfully gumming a wad of tobacco—no wonder he was toothless—and spittin' his nasty juice in a coffee can. In low voices we were continuing our conversation about Belle when Cassie suddenly held up one hand and jerked her head to the rear. We looked behind us, and there were the Lucky young'uns eavesdropping over the top of the seat.

The three of them simultaneously stuck purple tongues out at us. There were two girls and a boy, all with cornflower blue eyes and the dirtiest faces I ever did see on anything human. They had bushy white hair that they were scratching at one moment and pushing out of their eyes the next. All of them were sucking on grape Tootsie Pops, which explained the color of their tongues.

The boy had on worn-out overalls with galluses, and the girls had on matching dresses with big blue roses all over them. I had seen sacks of grain at the feed store with that design on them.

"Excuse us," I said to them politely. "We were having a private conversation here."

"'Scuse us," the boy said prissily, obviously imitating me. "We were having a private conversation here."

The three children belly-laughed. You'd think it was the funniest thing they'd ever heard. I was speechless, and I felt my face growing hot. I was not used to being made fun of.

"I warned you." Cassie leaned over close and whispered through clenched teeth. "I said not to give them one lick of attention."

"I warned you!" one of the Lucky girls mocked devilishly.

She was hanging her mangy head right down between me and Woodrow.

"Ignore them," Cassie whispered again.

"Ignore them!" the Lucky young'uns all said together.

It was clear they were going to repeat everything we said, and they were grinning like a bunch of possums. Lordy, what a nightmare, I was thinking. I searched for their mama, and there she was by herself a few seats behind us reading a *Modern Romances* magazine.

Woodrow, Cassie, and I went into a dead silence. If we'd had pencils and paper we could have passed notes; the Luckys probably couldn't read. But of course we didn't have any with us. We would just have to wait them out. They would get bored and leave to go find other mischief.

Wrong. They started kicking the back of our seat.

"You know what!" Woodrow said suddenly, and stood up.

He acted like he was so aggravated. The young'uns sat up grinning and looked at him.

"I really wanted to tell everybody a story!" he went on, and threw up his hands in exasperation. "But how can I hear myself think with all that racket, and banging on the seat? Can you tell me that?"

The grins faded away.

"A feller can't tell a story to save his life!"

And with that Woodrow sat down again in a huff.

A tousled head popped up over the top of the seat. It was the Lucky boy.

"A story 'bout whut?" he said.

Woodrow turned to him. "Whadda you care? You wouldn't listen to it. You'd just kick me in the head or something!"

"Naw, we won't kick ye no more if you'll tell us a story."

The other two heads came up over the seat.

"Not never no more?" Woodrow said.

All three heads bobbed up and down.

"Well, does that mean yes you will, or does it mean no you won't?" Woodrow said, huffy again.

Cassie and I giggled.

"It . . . it means yeah we won't kick ye no more," one of the girls said.

"All right, then," Woodrow said. "When you give your word, you know you gotta keep it? If you don't, you'll sprout horns like a billy goat."

I sneaked a peek at the mother, who was still glued to her magazine. She had escaped and wasn't about to come back yet.

Woodrow got up on his knees and faced the children. Cassie and I moved over to the empty seat behind Pap, because Woodrow needed a lot of room to tell a story right.

"This is a true story that my mama told me. It happened down in Kentucky. There was this boy, see, who would go out ever' day and play in the woods, and he could hear voices in the water running over the rocks, and in the wind, and he could see faces in the blossom of a flower, and not only that, but he could see tiny people running in and out among the briars and weeds. And they would giggle and beckon him to come play with them. So he did. And they would tell him and show him *fey* things."

Woodrow emphasized the word *fey*, then turned and grinned at Cassie.

"Then one day his little friend Ann died," Woodrow continued, "and he felt so bad that he went into the woods to cry."

The children were absorbed.

"And while he was there, a beautiful lady appeared to him. Her eyes were like the blue in a flame, and her hair was yella as corn. She wore a long shimmery gown, and had glass slippers on her feet, and—"

"It was Cinderella!" one of the girls said breathlessly.

"No! It was not Cinderella!" Woodrow said crankily. "Maybe they were silver slippers instead of glass. But it was *not* Cinderella. Anyway, she said to him, 'What's wrong, Eddie?' That was his name—Eddie.

"And Eddie told her what was wrong, so she said, 'Make any wish you so desire and I will grant it unto you.'

"So he told her that he would like to grow up to have the gift of healing people, especially children, because it made him sad to see young'uns suffer and die.

"And the beautiful lady said, 'Your wish is granted.'

"And she vanished into a cloud, and he was amazed. When Eddie grew up, he found out he could look inside of people and see what was wrong with them, and heal them. And he got famous; then he died."

"Couldn't he cure his own self?" the Lucky boy asked.

"No, he could not," Woodrow said, and then he asked, "Are y'all going to Bluefield?"

The three heads bobbed again, as the children looked at Woodrow with new respect.

"Well, lookee here," Woodrow said, and he showed them a nickel. "I'll give this buffalo to the one who can stay the quietest the rest of the trip."

We didn't hear another peep from the Luckys.

7 ◄

Our next stop was Deep Vale, which had a real depot with a diner. Woodrow and I started to follow Cassie inside, but before we got to the door, Woodrow caught sight of a rest room sign on the outside of the terminal.

"There," he said, and sprinted for that door. "I'll meet y'all inside."

"Oh, shucks!" Cassie said, and took off after him.

He had his hand on the door knob when she reached him and gave his arm a jerk.

"Woodrow, wait!"

Woodrow turned around, and I could see the annoyance on his face, because he was bustin' to go.

"What is it?" he said irritably.

"You don't want to go in there, Woodrow."

"Course I do!" he hollered.

"Just take a look at the sign there," Cassie said as she jerked her thumb toward the door.

"It says MEN," he said, exasperated.

"What does it say above that?" Cassie yelled.

He looked again.

"It says COLORED," he yelled back at her.

That stopped him short because Woodrow had never seen such a sign before.

"What does it mean?" he asked.

"It means white folks have their rest rooms inside the terminal. These here are for colored folks."

"Why?" Woodrow said.

Cassie shrugged. "I don't know, but that's the way it is. White folks have their rest rooms, and colored folks have theirs."

Disgruntled, Woodrow followed Cassie into the terminal and without another word went to the WHITE ONLY men's room, while Cassie and I went to the WHITE ONLY women's room. Then we met in the diner, perched on stools in front of the counter, and ordered hot cocoa.

"That'll be fifteen cents," the waitress said.

We hauled out our nickels and paid.

"Will we see any colored folks today?" Woodrow asked Cassie.

"I imagine so," she said.

"I never saw one in person before," Woodrow said, "but I'd like to."

"You never saw colored people?" Cassie said. "How about you, Gypsy?"

"Yeah, we always see them in Bristol when Mama takes me shopping there," I said.

"I've seen some in pictures in the paper," Woodrow said, "and in the movies and on television."

"Yonder's a colored boy now," Cassie said and pointed to a tall, gangly teenage boy outside the window. He was wearing a brilliant jacket of red, green, and black Scotch plaid.

"A real colored person," Woodrow said with wonder all over his face. "And look at that snappy jacket, will ya? Ain't that the best-looking thing you ever laid eyes on?"

When we got on our bus to continue the trip, we caught a glimpse of that bright plaid at the rear of the bus, and there was the colored boy at one end of the last seat, which ran the width of the bus.

"Maybe we can get him to come up here and sit with us," Woodrow said in an excited whisper.

"I don't think so," Cassie said as she took the seat behind Pap again.

"Why not?" Woodrow asked.

"It's the law," Cassie said in a low voice. "Coloreds have to sit in the back of the bus."

Pap climbed into the driver's seat and stuck up one thumb to Cassie, which was his signal to her that we were ready to move on. Then he started the engine.

"Next stop is Bluefield!" Cassie announced.

Woodrow couldn't keep his mind or his eyes off the colored boy.

"Maybe we should go and talk to him," he said after a while. "He's all by his lonesome."

"Woodrow," I said. "You go talk to him if you wanna. There's no law against *that*."

"Why don't y'all come with me?" Woodrow said.

"If we all three go together, it'll scare 'im," Cassie said. "He'll think we're gonna hurt him."

"Why would he think that?" Woodrow asked.

"Well, some people are just plain mean," Cassie said, "and when they catch a colored person alone, they gang up on him."

"It's in the paper all the time, Woodrow," I said. "Don't you ever read what's going on in other places?"

"Yeah," Woodrow said, "but I don't pay much attention, because things like that don't seem real to me. They happen somewhere else. They don't happen in my world. It's like reading about the cowboys and Indians in the frontier days."

The boy had taken off the plaid jacket, and was sitting there in a long-sleeved green flannel shirt that was open at the neck. He was staring out the window, deep in thought.

"I'm going to talk to him," Woodrow said, suddenly determined. "Come on, girls, go with me. He won't be scared of us. It's broad daylight and there's other people around."

Cassie and I looked at each other and reluctantly agreed. Nearly everybody stared at us as we stood up and approached the colored boy. He watched us suspiciously.

"Hey there, what'cha doin'?" Woodrow greeted him as friendly as could be.

"Doin' nothin'," he replied, looking us over. "Whadda you want?"

"Nothin'," Woodrow said as he perched on the center of the long seat, and Cassie and I took the other end. "I never saw a colored boy in person before, and I thought I'd just say hey."

"Say what?" the boy snapped, with a combination of anger and disbelief. "You never saw *what*?"

"A colored boy," Woodrow replied innocently. "Nor any colored person. Never saw one before. Never did, and that's the truth."

"Huh!" the boy grunted. "Colored? You still ain't seen one!"

"Meaning what?" Woodrow said.

"I mean colored is red and green and yellow and blue. This skin here . . ." He held out a hand to demonstrate. "This skin is black! It ain't colored! It's black!"

"Well, it looks more brown to me," Woodrow said,

and it was the truth. "To me it looks about the color of a pecan."

Now, people in our neck of the woods were in the habit of pronouncing that word PEE-can because that's how we had always heard it said.

But apparently we were wrong, because the boy said knowingly, "I think what you want to say is pe-CAN. You say CAN harder than pee. A pe-CAN is a nut. They grow 'em in Georgia. A PEE-can is something you put under your bed at night."

"Well, shut my mouth," Woodrow said.

And that's just what he did. What can you say after a speech like that? So we rode along in silence for a minute, then Woodrow thought of a retort.

"Well, my skin's not white either!" he said. "Just look at it!" Woodrow spread one hand out flat against his thigh. "I'd say that skin there is more the color of . . . Now, what would you call it?"

"An English walnut!" the boy said as quick as that. "Your skin is the color of an English walnut."

"Hmmm," Woodrow muttered, studying his own hand. "An English walnut, huh? Well, I guess that makes us just a couple of nuts, don't it?"

Cassie and I giggled, but the boy didn't crack a smile. He was ignoring us and sizing Woodrow up.

"We want to be called black," he said then, real serious.

"Okay, black it is," Woodrow said.

He touched the material of the plaid jacket, which was folded neatly on the seat between him and the boy.

"I sure do like this," Woodrow said.

At once the boy snatched the coat up and stuffed it between himself and the window.

Woodrow was not discouraged. "That's what I said to my cousin Gypsy and our friend Cassie here, when we first saw you," he went on. "I said you looked snappy as all get-out."

Woodrow gestured to us as he said our names, and the boy glanced our way.

"Hey," we said, and he nodded at us.

"Did your mama buy you that coat?" Woodrow asked.

"My mama's dead."

"Oh. What about your daddy?"

"He's dead, too."

"Then who do you live with?" Woodrow probed, but the boy didn't answer. Instead, he turned and stared out the window.

"What's your name?" Woodrow plowed on.

"Joseph." He answered that one. "Joseph Lincoln. What's yours?"

"I'm Woodrow Prater. Where you from, Joseph?"

"Asheville, North Carolina," Joseph replied, "and I'm on my way to Bluefield, West Virginia."

"We're going to Bluefield, too. How old are you, Joseph?"

"Me? I'm . . . well, I'm fifteen, almost sixteen."

Joseph pulled his frame up as big as it would go and looked down his nose at us. "How old are *y'all*?" he said.

"I'm thirteen, and so's Gypsy," Woodrow said. Then he laid a hand on Cassie's arm and added, "And Cassie here is a wee lass, but she's older than the hills."

Cassie laughed good-naturedly, but Joseph remained stone-faced.

"What are you going to Bluefield for?" Woodrow asked.

Joseph ignored Woodrow's question again but asked one of his own. "How come you never saw black people before? Did'ja grow up in a cave?"

"Just about," Woodrow replied. "I spent my whole life in a real backward place—Crooked Ridge, Virginia. Never been anywhere else but Coal Station, and it's just a wide place in the road. I live there now with Grandpa and Granny. But my grandpa is gonna take me to Baltimore, Maryland, in about a month."

Joseph said nothing.

"You wanna know why we're going to Baltimore?" Woodrow said.

"Why?"

"He's taking me to a famous hospital. It's called Johns Hopkins. A doctor there is gonna look at my eyes and see if he can make 'em straight."

Woodrow pushed up his glasses, and didn't even blink

as Joseph squinted into his face, and examined his crossed eyes.

"Have you ever been to Baltimore?" Woodrow asked.

Joseph shook his head.

"I guess you're in the ninth grade now, Joseph?"

"No, I'm in the seventh . . ." Joseph said. He paused. Then the hardness of his face melted. "Okay, Woodrow, you caught me. I lied about my age 'cause people say I look older'n I am. I'm just thirteen, too."

"Well, you sure had us fooled," Woodrow said. "Didn't he, girls?"

Woodrow turned to me and Cassie. We nodded.

"Are you going to an orphanage?" was Woodrow's next question to Joseph.

"No, I am not!" Joseph said emphatically.

"Well, I know you can't live by yourself," Woodrow said. "There's a law against it—or something."

"I was living with that stinkin' Roosevelt Hale!" Joseph said.

"Was?" from Woodrow.

"See, I have a brother named Ethan," Joseph started explaining, "and after Mama died two months ago, Ethan had to make a living for us 'cause he's sixteen and he could get a job where I couldn't. We had no more kin nearby to do for us, but I thought we were doing just fine by ourselves.

"Then Ethan got a chance to go to California with his

buddies, so he dropped me off at Roosevelt Hale's, who was no more to us than a neighbor we'd hardly ever spoke to before. And Ethan left me there with nothing but a few clothes and a ten-dollar bill. He told me he would send for me someday."

Joseph paused and swallowed hard.

"*Someday?*" Joseph's voice broke on the word. "What does that mean? A whole month went by and he didn't even write. Next thing I knew, Roosevelt had my coat hanging with his own things. Said he would keep it 'safe' for me. Safe, huh! He aimed to have it for his own self. I knew that!

"He made me do all the work at his place . . . to earn my room and board, he said. And if I didn't do it, he'd whoop me."

I entered the conversation. "Gee, that sounds like the Joseph in the Bible, who was sold into slavery by his brothers."

"You're right!" Woodrow exclaimed. "And he had a coat of many colors, too!"

"Can you interpret dreams?" Cassie asked him. "Like the Joseph in the Bible?"

Joseph shook his head.

"Well, I can," Cassie announced proudly. "So if you have a dream you want interpretated, you just let me know."

For the first time Joseph showed some interest in somebody besides Woodrow.

"Where did you learn how to do that?" he asked Cassie.

Cassie shrugged. "I don't know. I've always known."

"Did you run away from that stinkin' feller?" Woodrow went on with his interrogation.

"Yeah, I did," Joseph said. "Yesterday, while he was at work, I pulled my ten-dollar bill out of its hiding place, took my coat from Roosevelt's closet, and headed to the bus station."

"And what're you gonna do in Bluefield?" Woodrow wanted to know.

Again Joseph ignored the question. Nobody said anything for a spell, and Woodrow certainly could not put up with that.

"Let me tell you about *my* mama," he blurted out, emphasizing *my* like it was the most important word in his sentence. "She just disappeared."

He crossed his arms, looked at Joseph, and waited for the inevitable reaction. He was not disappointed.

"Whadda ya mean?" Joseph said, perking up all over.

"Well, me and my daddy, we got up one morning and she was gone. That's all. Nobody's seen her since."

"But you don't mean like *poof*!" Joseph said, snapping his fingers. "And she vanished into thin air?"

"Prob'ly not, but we didn't see her go," Woodrow said. "So we don't know what happened."

Then Woodrow abbreviated the story about his mother for Joseph, added the New Year's Eve phone call, and told him what we were planning to do in Bluefield.

"No foolin'?" Joseph said, and you could tell he was immediately sucked into the Belle Prater mystery, just like everybody else.

"Here's a picture of her," Woodrow said and drew the snapshot from his pocket. Joseph looked at it and handed it back without commenting.

"Wanna come along and help?" Woodrow asked Joseph hopefully.

"I reckon so" was Joseph's surprising reply.

And the Belle Prater search team grew to four.

8

The sky had darkened by the time we got to Bluefield. Pap removed suitcases from the luggage bin under
the bus, and Cassie answered the passengers' questions
as they disembarked. Woodrow, Joseph, and I stood outside the door, waiting for her to finish up.

As the toothless man passed he said, "Now, you
young'uns don't forget to read the signs!"

We assured him we would not forget, and he struck
off walking down the street.

The Lucky brats appeared and paused beside Woodrow, while their mama barged on, still lost in her own
world.

"That's right, I promised somebody a nickel, didn't I?"
Woodrow said.

The children were all eyes as Woodrow rummaged
around in his pocket and pulled out a handful of coins.
He was always proud to show off how much money he

had these days. Before coming to live with Granny and Grandpa, he never had two nickels to rub together.

"It was nearabout impossible to tell who was the best," Woodrow said, as he plucked three nickels from the change. "So I've got one for everybody, how's that?"

The children grinned as they took their nickels and ran to catch up with their mama.

Woodrow turned to Joseph. "Don't you have to be somewhere at a certain time?"

"Don't worry 'bout it," Joseph mumbled. "I got time to help you look for your mama."

Cassie kissed Pap goodbye, and said to us, "Let's fly."

Taking our cue from Cassie, we all acted like we had wings. Chirping and flapping our arms, we swooped down on Bluefield and landed on a corner, where we stopped and looked around.

It was a pleasant, cozy town with sidewalks running along in front of neatly painted houses, and big old oak trees growing beside paved streets. It seemed like a place you could snuggle up in.

On the next block there was a homey eatery with a red-and-white-striped awning over the entrance. The front window was filled with cute baskets of fruit, and on the glass were the words JILL'S CAFÉ.

"Let's go in here and get something to eat first of all," Woodrow said. "It's nearly lunchtime, and I'm starved."

Woodrow was always starved. Grandpa said he had hollow legs.

When we started to go in, Joseph said, "I'll just wait out here."

"What for?" Woodrow said.

Joseph pointed to a sign: WHITE ONLY.

"We'll find another place," I said quickly.

"They're all alike," Cassie said. "Gypsy, let's you and me go in and get everybody's food and bring it out here."

"Yeah, and I'll stay with Joseph," Woodrow said.

Nobody mentioned that it was too cold to eat outside, but that hateful sign left us no choice.

"You can get me a hot dog and some pop in a cup," Joseph said to me, and handed me a quarter.

"Same for me," Woodrow said, and gave me a quarter as well.

So Cassie and I went in together, placed the orders, then carried them outside. Woodrow and Joseph had found a bench at a bus stop, and we huddled together with our food, girls in the middle and a boy at each end of the bench.

For a while we were too busy eating to talk. Before long, over the noisy smacking of our lips, we heard Woodrow say, "Joseph, you workin' for the FBI?"

"No!" Joseph replied with a laugh. "Why'd you ask me that?"

"I thought maybe that's why you can't tell us what you're doing here," Woodrow said. "Maybe it's top secret."

"Woodrow!" I snapped at him. "Maybe it's personal!"

"No, it's okay," Joseph said with a big sigh. He must have figured Woodrow was not going to let up. And he was right. "You see . . ."

Joseph studied his fingernails like he saw something interesting there. He picked a piece of lint off his jacket and stared across the street at a house where a refrigerator was being delivered. I knew he was searching for the right words. Even Woodrow managed not to hurry him.

Joseph tried again. "You see . . . my daddy . . ."

He stalled again.

"Your daddy's dead, right?" I tried to help him.

"Not exactly," Joseph said.

"*Not exactly* means he's alive, right?" Cassie said.

"Mama always told us we should think of him as dead, but he's not really," Joseph said.

"Is he in a coma?" Woodrow said.

"No, he's not in a coma!" Joseph said, and laughed again. "Woodrow, you really are a nut, you know that?" Then he went on quickly, running all his words together, "MydaddydisappearedtooonlyitwaswhenIwasababy. HedesertedMamaandmeandEthan."

Silently we unscrambled his words and absorbed them.

"And you still don't know where he's at?" Cassie said at last.

"I didn't for a long time, but two Christmases ago, he sent me this coat, and Ethan a watch. It was the first and last time we heard from him in all those years."

Joseph put his hand into the pocket of his coat and brought out a tiny brown scrap of paper. He sat there staring at it.

"Mama let us keep the presents, but she threw away the package, because his address was on it. Later I dug it out of the trash, and tore away this corner where the address was printed. I've been carrying it around ever since."

"Did you write him?" I said.

"I wrote about twenty letters," Joseph said. "But I tore them all up. Never mailed a one. I was afraid."

"Afraid of what?" Cassie said. "He's your daddy, ain't he?"

"Yeah, but what if . . ." Joseph started and stopped.

"I know how you feel," Woodrow interjected. "After all, he deserted you."

"Yeah, but then he sent the Christmas package with this address on it, like he was trying to reach out."

"The same with Mama's anonymous phone call," Woodrow said. "You just don't know what to think, do you?"

We were each inside our own thoughts as we finished eating in silence.

"So what's the address?" Cassie asked after a while. She reached for the scrap of paper in Joseph's hand and read aloud, "One-eleven Appalachian Street, Bluefield, West Virginia."

For a split second I guess I absorbed some of Cassie's talent for seeing into the future, because I knew what she was going to say next.

"I know exactly where that's at, Joseph. It's on the other side of town, but this is a small town, so it's not far."

"Well, let's go! Let's go!" Woodrow cried, jumping to his feet. "We gotta get started. Now we got two people to find."

We left the bench and headed in the direction of Appalachian Street, agreeing to ask people about Aunt Belle along the way, and show her picture. Joseph suggested we take our time and do a thorough search. He wanted to tag along with us and shore up his confidence before going to his daddy's door. He was nervous.

"I don't know what scares me most—finding him and him telling me to go away, or not finding him at all."

I was proud that he now felt comfortable enough to confide in us.

"What are you going to do if he's not there?" Woodrow asked.

Joseph shrugged and tried to be nonchalant. "Oh, I don't know. I'll prob'ly strike out for California to find Ethan."

Nobody said what they thought of that plan.

"I know," Joseph said after a few moments. His shoulders slumped. "It's stupid."

"Have you thought of calling your daddy?" Woodrow said.

"Yeah, I tried to get his number from Information," Joseph said. "But they didn't have it. Maybe he's got no phone."

"Or maybe he's not here anymore," Cassie said.

"Yeah, thanks, Cassie," Joseph said glumly.

"Sorry," Cassie mumbled.

We soon found ourselves in the midst of a congested business district for the next several blocks, and a lot of people were in the streets.

The first place we stopped was at a movie theater. *The Country Girl*, with Grace Kelly, was playing. We showed the ticket seller Aunt Belle's picture and asked if she had seen this lady. No luck. Next we went to a department store, then a grocery store, a drugstore, a couple of cafés, a post office, a bank, and more stores, but the only thing we learned was that most people couldn't care less. Some of them were rude to Joseph, and he started waiting outside for us when we went into a place. We felt bad about that, so Cassie and I took turns waiting with him.

Then came the freezing rain, so that we were not only cold but wet on top of it. You can't get more uncomfortable than that, and being in a strange town somehow made it worse. Tomorrow, I thought, with a feeling I imagined to be homesickness, I can spend the whole day curled up on the couch in front of the fireplace, reading Nancy Drew, with Mama and Porter close by.

My eyes fell on Joseph's thirteen-year-old face, which was old with worry. If he didn't find his daddy, what would he be doing tomorrow? Where would he go? He had no family near, and no one he could call for help.

If a white boy was in a strange town in Joseph's predicament, he could go to the police and they would help him. But a black boy? Well, they were liable to throw him in the jailhouse, or something worse.

"I didn't know how hard it would be," Woodrow admitted sadly, as we were taking shelter under an overhanging storefront. "And I didn't count on this weather."

"Let's go directly to Appalachian Street," I suggested. I started to add, "Then we can return to the bus station," but decided against it.

"Okay," Woodrow agreed. "Maybe the rain will let up and we can do some more searching later."

I was thinking how nice it would be if we were invited inside at the Appalachian Street address to warm up and dry out. We left our shelter, with Cassie leading the way and Joseph beside her on the sidewalk. Woodrow and I followed.

"Don't you think it's strange," Woodrow said to me,

"that we should run into a boy who is also looking for one of his parents today, just like I am?"

"I guess so."

"I think it's a sign. Don't you think it's funny how that old man kept talking about signs?"

"It was hilarious," I said.

"No, I don't mean funny ha-ha. I mean odd."

"And how's that?"

"He kept saying, 'Read the signs!'"

"He was repetitious all right."

In front of us Cassie and Joseph stopped at a corner. Uh-oh, another sign. This one read Appalachian Street. Joseph seemed nailed to the sidewalk, but Cassie forged ahead, searching house numbers.

"Here it is!" she called from a few houses down. "One-eleven. And it says *Lincoln* on the mailbox."

It was a small green house with white shutters. There was a wide wooden porch, and the front door was in the center with a window on each side. You could see the glow of a lamp through lace curtains.

"Go on," Woodrow encouraged Joseph. "If anything goes wrong, well . . . we'll be waiting ri'cheer."

Joseph crossed the patch of yard to the front steps. When he glanced over his shoulder, we could not read his face. Then he abruptly made a U-turn and came back to where we stood.

"I'm scared," he said. "What if he don't want to see me? What if he's mean?"

"Why don't we all go to the door and ask for directions?" I said. "We can say we are lost and we have to find our way to the bus station."

"That's good," Woodrow agreed.

"So we get directions, then what?" Cassie said.

"We say how cold we are," Woodrow said.

"And maybe somebody will invite us in to get warm?" I said hopefully.

"Maybe so," Joseph said. "Then what?"

But nobody had an answer for him.

"Joseph, you do the talking," Woodrow said. "Whoever answers the door may be suspicious of English walnuts."

We all followed Joseph across the yard and up the steps. As we reached the door, it opened. A very tiny gray-headed black woman, dressed in a neat blue housedress, peeped around the door. Not one of us had ever seen a midget before, not face-to-face anyhow, but there she was.

"What'n the world can I do for you?" she chirped in a nasal and childlike voice.

Joseph could do nothing but stare at the little woman. He was tongue-tied. It was plain he was going to be worthless in this project, and much to my surprise, Woodrow was not faring any better.

"We're lost," I spoke up. "Maybe you can help us out?"

The woman's eyes flitted from Joseph to me, back to Joseph, then to me again before she spoke. "Like the old song goes, 'I once was lost, but now I'm found.' What're you looking for?"

"I'm so-ooo cold!" Cassie suddenly blurted out, as she wrapped her arms around herself. "It's freezin' out here."

The wee lady looked at her and Woodrow then, paused for only a moment, and without a word stood aside and held the door open for us. Cassie, Woodrow, and I had to squeeze past Joseph to get in, for he was still in a state of shock and had not moved. Only when he was left standing there alone did he come to his senses.

"Much obliged," he mumbled, and entered the house behind us.

Just like the woman, the room was tiny but very warm and inviting. At one glance my eyes took in the lace curtains, a cozy overstuffed sofa and armchair to match, bookcases lining one wall, and best of all, a fireplace roaring with flames.

"This feels good," Cassie said, rubbing her hands together before the blaze.

Woodrow, Joseph, and I joined her.

The woman closed the door and stood against it. I figured she did not know what to make of us, but the feeling was mutual.

"This is real nice of you," I said. "We're awful cold."

Her eyes rested on me, but she still said nothing. I realized that with my shoes and pants splashed with mud, and my hair dripping into my eyes, I was just one of the gang. Joseph, in his fine Scottish coat, was the one who might be considered overdressed now.

Cassie introduced herself.

"And I am *Miz* Lincoln, as my students used to say. I'm a retired teacher."

She emphasized the word *Miz*. That's what all kids called their teachers. And there was that name Lincoln. Joseph's expression was unreadable, but he could not take his eyes off her.

Woodrow and I said our names, then everybody turned to Joseph.

"Jo . . . Joseph," he said.

"No last name?" Miz Lincoln said.

"Just Joseph," he repeated softly.

Miz Lincoln studied his face curiously.

"How's about some hot tea?" she said to him.

"Oh yes, ma'am, we'd like that," Joseph answered.

"Then y'all sit down, and I'll start the water to boil."

With those words, she left the room.

"Wow, a real honest-to-God midget!" Woodrow whispered.

"Yeah," I said, and turned to Joseph. "Who do you reckon she is?"

Joseph just shook his head and looked into the fire.

Miz Lincoln reentered the room, carrying a tray that held a creamer, a sugar bowl, a dish of sliced lemons, cups, and spoons. Shortly we were all settled on a rug before the fire, sipping our tea. Our coats were in a pile by the hearth, except for Joseph's. He had insisted on keeping his on.

Miz Lincoln was sitting on the sofa, her small slip-
pered feet dangling, her arms crossed over her chest,
quietly observing us.

"Uh . . . 'scuse me," Woodrow said politely, "but
something's the matter with my tea."

We all looked into Woodrow's cup, and sure enough it
looked funny. There were clouds floating in it.

"Did you put lemon in it?" Miz Lincoln asked him.

"Yes, ma'am."

"And did you put milk in it, too?"

"Yes, ma'am."

"Well, there you have it. You've clabbered the milk.
Lemon and milk don't mix, my boy."

"Oh" was all Woodrow said as Miz Lincoln took his
cup. You could tell he felt embarrassed.

"One of life's small lessons for you," she said kindly.
"It's a thing everybody's gotta learn sooner or later. Isn't
it nice to get it over with?"

She took Woodrow's cup into the kitchen, returned
with a clean one, and poured a fresh cup of tea for him.
He added only milk this time.

Miz Lincoln turned to Joseph. "I've been looking at
that god-awful coat," she said. "Where did you buy it?"

I'll have to say that startled us all good and proper. I
thought I saw some temper in Joseph's eyes, but he answered polite enough, "My daddy bought me this coat."

"Well, I might look like a clown, but I'm no dummy,"

she said bluntly. "And that's the ugliest coat ever made. Your daddy's got no taste. Who might he be anyhow?"

Joseph was completely dumbfounded.

"And where'd you get this team of yours?" she went on, making a sweeping gesture toward me, Woodrow, and Cassie.

"I . . . I m-met up with them on the way here," Joseph stammered. "They were f-friendly to me."

"Where are y'all from?"

"I'm from Asheville, North Carolina," Joseph said.

"And we're from Coal Station," Woodrow said.

But Miz Lincoln seemed not to hear Woodrow.

"I am your Aunt Carlotta, your father's sister," she said to Joseph.

"My father's what?"

At that Miz Lincoln busted out laughing.

"Didn't anybody ever tell you there was a midget in the family?"

Joseph shook his head slowly.

"I'm adopted," she explained. "I'm a good bit older than Reeve, and I practically raised him by myself."

"Reeve?" Joseph repeated the name.

"Yeah, Reeve Lincoln, your old man. I think your mother called him Linc. Most folks do."

"That's right," Joseph said. "Where's he at anyhow?"

"I wish I knew, honeybunch. I've seen neither hide nor hair of that scoundrel for almost two years."

I O ◄

Miz Lincoln motioned Joseph to come over and sit by her on the couch, which he did, and she commenced telling her and Reeve's story.

"I was born to normal-sized parents with pea-sized brains. They took one look at my 'deformity' and yelled for somebody to come and take this monstrosity away. They didn't have sense enough to realize that a deformity, like beauty, is in the eye of the beholder. You may not know it, but there are many like me born every year to all races of people. Most people call us midgets or dwarfs, but we prefer to be called Little People.

"Your Grandma and Grandpa Lincoln didn't have children of their own at that time, and they wanted me, Joseph. They really wanted me!"

Miz Lincoln had a big beaming smile on her face when she said that.

"It was probably the luckiest break I ever got. They

loved me, and took care of me, and treated me like I was as big as anybody. Why, they made me feel like I was five feet tall—ha! That's a joke."

We all laughed to be polite.

"Did you ever see Little People in the public schools?" Miz Lincoln asked us. "No, you didn't. There was no such thing, then or now. So I was educated at home, and it was no inferior education, either. My mama knew what she was doing.

"Then when I was fifteen, my little brother, Reeve, was born. He was really something. We just about loved him to pieces.

"When I was seventeen, I went away to a special college where there were others like me, and I studied to become a teacher, but I don't know what for. After I graduated, the regular schools wouldn't hire me. So I moved home and just bided my time, hanging around the house for a few months. And then, out of the clear blue sky, both of my adopted parents got killed in a car wreck. It was the worst time of my whole life, but for Reeve's sake, I had to pull myself together and go on. Somehow I had to support the two of us.

"Since no other school wanted me, I got me a job teaching circus children. Circuses and carnivals have always been a sanctuary for misfits like me who might be considered freaks. Some of my students were actually performers, but a lot of them were the sons and daughters of the barkers, animal trainers, high-wire walkers, flying trapeze artists, jugglers, and of course the clowns, who were mostly Little People like me. I had finally found a place where I could feel I belonged. They saw nothing odd about me. Reeve and I traveled all over the country with them for years. And we had the time of our lives.

"But sometime during that period with the circus, Reeve took up gambling—or, I should say, it took him. When he turned eighteen, he left me and he left the circus and struck out hitchhiking to wherever the road would lead him. He has been a wanderer and a gambler ever since. I never knew where he was from one day to the next, except for those years he was married to your mother."

"A wanderer? A gambler?" Joseph echoed.

"I'm afraid so. He's plain addicted to gambling. Try as he will to quit, he can't seem to do it. To him it's like smoking cigarettes, and I think he's tried every trick known to give it up, but he's failed.

"When he met your mama, he fell head over heels in love. She had a way about her that settled him, calmed him, and kept him by the home fires. It was the incentive he needed to quit, and he did—for a while, anyway. Then he started gambling again.

"At this point things got ugly. His addiction made him steal food from y'all and take clothes off your backs.

When he lost the house . . . well, that's when he hit the road again. He was doing you a favor."

"What house?"

"Your mother never told you?"

"No. She never talked about him at all. She said we should consider him dead."

"I can understand that," Miz Lincoln said sadly. "But I wonder why she never told you about me. I always liked your mama, Joseph."

Joseph had no answer for her.

"Anyway," she went on, "when you were just a baby, your mother and father owned a house together in Asheville, and he gambled it away."

"No foolin'?" Joseph said. "A whole house?"

"A whole house," Miz Lincoln said, and shook her head slowly, as if she still couldn't believe it. "When he left you, he wandered around some more, gambled some more. Then two years ago he figured he had hit rock bottom and couldn't sink any lower. He longed to be clean again. So right in the midst of this big old horse race, he took to praying.

"'Lord,' he said, 'if you let me win this last bet, I will never gamble again, and the only thing I will try to win from now on is respect.'

"Reeve told me later that it was against all odds, all logic, all reason that his horse would win that race, but it did. And he took it as a sign from God."

Woodrow nudged me and whispered, "Read the signs."

"Your father was as good as his word, Joseph," Miz Lincoln continued. "He quit gambling for the second time. By then I had retired from the circus, bought this house for my golden years, and settled down. He came here and asked could he stay with me while he was trying to pull his life together. Natur'ly I couldn't turn him down. Never could. Besides, I was happy to have him.

"He got himself an honest job doing construction work. And with some of the money from that last bet, your father bought a watch for Ethan, and that fine coat for you, Joseph."

Here Miz Lincoln grinned and poked Joseph in the chest with her index finger. "I was joshin' you about that coat, lad. I was the one who picked it out."

Joseph broke into a big grin his own self, and I was glad to see it. I figured right then he was going to be all right.

"Yeah, I took one look at that coat," Miz Lincoln continued, "and I says to myself, says I, 'That's it! That's a fine coat for my nephew Joseph.' And I mailed it and the watch to y'all at Christmas, along with the letter."

Joseph's head shot up. "What letter?"

"There was a letter to you and Ethan from your daddy in that package. If your mama didn't give it to you, well, I can't fault her for that, either."

"What did the letter say?"

"He asked your forgiveness and asked if he could come and see you."

"But he never got an answer, did he?" Joseph said.

"No," Miz Lincoln said sadly. "And it was just as well. He couldn't stay clean. Gambling is a powerful addiction. He didn't last six months."

"So when I came to your door," Joseph said, "did you know me by the coat?"

"Yes, I did. The minute I saw that coat, I said a silent prayer, 'Thank you, God, for bringing this boy to me.' How did you get here?"

"Came on a bus," Joseph said.

"Did you run away from home?"

"Not really," Joseph said.

"Then your mother knows where you are?"

It was then that I saw in Joseph's dark eyes the grief that he had so carefully concealed from us until this moment.

"Mama died the last of October," he said in a quivering voice.

I felt a hot stinging behind my own eyelids.

"Oh, I can't tell you how sorry I am, Joseph," said Miz Lincoln as she touched his arm. "How did she die?"

"Heart attack."

"Tell me about it."

Joseph told his story with lots of feeling, specially

when he came to the part where Ethan dumped him at the home of a man he hardly knew.

"Your father first, then Ethan abandoned you, too," his aunt said softly.

"Ethan and me, we coulda made it together," Joseph said. "But I couldn't make it by myself."

"Course not," Miz Lincoln said sympathetically. "But you and me, Joseph? I'm sure we'll do just fine."

For a minute there was no sound except for the crackling of wood in the fire and the ticking of a miniature grandfather clock on the mantel. The rain had slowed.

"I don't want to be a burden to you, Aunt Carlotta," Joseph said.

"A burden?" his aunt said with a funny, strangled sound that was a cross between a laugh and a sob. "My boy, you couldn't be a burden to me if you worked at it. Don't you know the years I spent caring for your father were my happiest? Having you here will be like having him with me again. It will give my life new meaning. Besides, I have a bedroom all ready for you."

"A bedroom?" Joseph said. "For me?"

"Yes, I had it papered with cowboys and Indians for you and Ethan. I was hoping you two would come looking for your daddy or me someday. Now you, at least, are here to stay."

Joseph glanced around the living room. I wondered

what he thought of his new home. Was he thinking he was safe at last? Was he imagining what it would be like to live here, and maybe see his father someday?

"I'm sure Reeve will contact me eventually, Joseph," Miz Lincoln said, "and we can tell him you're here. You can decide if you want to see him or not. Whatever you decide, you will always have a home with me."

Woodrow went to the window and looked out. The rain was still pouring down. He glanced at his watch, then resettled himself beside me in front of the fire. I was relieved he did not suggest going out into the weather again.

Miz Lincoln invited us to have an early supper with her, and presently we found ourselves seated around her table, enjoying a pot of navy beans, with cole slaw, corn bread, and butter. Woodrow, Cassie, and I made pure tee pigs of ourselves, but I noticed that Joseph merely picked at his food. I imagined he had too much emotion in him to taste anything proper. He didn't say much at all, but he hung on to every word his aunt said.

"So why did you kids come into Bluefield today?" Miz Lincoln finally turned her attention to me and Woodrow and Cassie.

Woodrow began his story once more. As we sat around the table listening to my cousin again recalling the mysterious disappearance of his mother, it occurred to me that he was able to speak about the whole episode now like he was talking about somebody else. In the beginning, when Woodrow's hurt was still fresh, he had been as pained as Joseph had been in describing his mother's death.

"And that's why we are here," Woodrow finished. "We thought it shouldn't be so hard to find her in a small place like this, but we haven't had any luck."

Then he brought out the photograph of his mama and handed it to Miz Lincoln. She pulled a pair of glasses from her apron pocket, placed them on her nose, and studied Aunt Belle's face. All was quiet for a moment as we watched her heavy brows go into a frown.

"She looks familiar," she said at last, and it was like a mild explosion in the quiet room.

"No kidding?" Woodrow said breathlessly.

Miz Lincoln propped the picture up beside her water glass and scrutinized it carefully.

"You said the story was big news at the time?" Miz Lincoln asked.

"Yeah, it was in all the papers," Woodrow said.

"Then it's possible that I saw her picture in the paper," Miz Lincoln said thoughtfully. "But I don't always read the newspaper, and I'll declare, I can't recall reading about this. I am sure I would remember such a story."

Woodrow moved quietly from his chair and went to stand behind Miz Lincoln to look over her shoulder, but

he didn't breathe for fear of disturbing her concentration.

"It's also possible that I saw her somewhere," the
woman mumbled at last, then turned to Woodrow and
said, "Could you leave the photo with me?"

Woodrow glanced toward the window again, and said,
"I guess so. It seems like the rain is never gonna let up, so
I won't need it anymore today. And I got plenty more at
home."

I breathed a sigh of relief.

Miz Lincoln produced a pencil from the drawer of a
nearby sideboard and asked Woodrow to write down the
number where he could be reached. Woodrow scribbled
Grandpa's phone number on the back of the snapshot.

"If you remember anything," he said to Miz Lincoln,
"call and let me know. Be sure and call collect. Grandpa
will be happy to pay."

Shortly after four o'clock Woodrow, Cassie, and I
pulled on our coats, preparing to walk to the bus station.
Miz Lincoln, however, insisted on calling a taxi for us
and paying the fare herself. She said children shouldn't
be running around in freezing rain, in near darkness, in a
strange place, and I sure was glad she felt that way.

When the taxi arrived, Joseph thanked us for helping
him, and we were all kinda awkward and tongue-tied
saying goodbye to him and Miz Lincoln.

"I want to come searching again next Saturday," Woodrow told them as we were going out the door. "Maybe I'll see you then."

"What do you mean, 'maybe'?" Miz Lincoln said. "If you come to Bluefield, you better come by and see us, or we'll be mad, won't we, Joseph?"

"That's right!" Joseph called after us. "We'll be mad!"

Then we waved at the two of them standing in the doorway together, as Cassie climbed into the taxi, with me following her, and Woodrow behind me.

We were quiet on the way to the bus station. Woodrow turned his eyes toward the soggy town with its big oaks and cozy houses all in neat rows. Darkness was creeping over everything, and you could see lights burning behind the windows, and you knew it was warm and dry inside. You could probably smell supper in there, and you could hear children laughing or bickering, singing or whining.

Woodrow was whispering, more to himself than to us. "Maybe she *is* here somewhere, behind one of these doors."

Several of the same people we had traveled with in the morning were on the bus going home. There was the big old woman with the pipe and June Honaker with her baby. When the Luckys got on the bus, I could see that their mama had been crying, and the kids didn't look too happy, either. The toothless man must have stayed on in Bluefield with his sister, Tulip.

There were also some newcomers, including two pretty ladies we knew as Tootsie and Ruby, who lived in Coal Station, and a young man named Chester.

Again Woodrow and I grabbed the wide seat at the end of the bus, and once we were on the road, Cassie joined us. There was a strong smell of fumes from the fuel of that old black-and-white bus, but right then it felt and smelled like home. It was warm and cozy in there 'cause it had a real good heater, while outside freezing rain was falling.

It was pitch black by the time the bus pulled out of the Bluefield terminal heading toward Deep Vale, and we were too give out to talk. Besides, there seemed nothing left to say.

Then, right on the outskirts of town, we saw some people huddled beside the road in the headlights, flagging the bus, and we came to life.

"They got *git*-tars!" Woodrow cried out. "And fiddles!"

"Oh, goody!" Cassie said. "It's the Bluegrass Blues!"

She hurried up front to welcome the musicians aboard, collect their fares, and guide them to the seats right in front of ours. There was a man and three women, which was not your ordinary bluegrass band. They were usually all men. Pap turned on the inside lights in the bus while Cassie helped the musicians store their instruments in the rack over the seats.

"What are they doing out'cheer on a night like this?" Woodrow said to Cassie when she returned to us.

"It's Saturday, and they're going to Deep Vale to play at a honky-tonk," she whispered. "We'll let them rest and warm up a bit. Then we'll ask them to play us some music. They're always glad to oblige."

Woodrow and I were squirming with excitement.

Pap had left the lights on, probably because he knew what was coming. Sure enough, about ten minutes later the one man in the band peeped around the side of his seat and said to Cassie, "Well, okay, my gal, I'll wager you wanna hear a tune, don'tcha?"

"I do!" Cassie said. "I wanna hear a tune, Billy Blue!"

Billy was a short, friendly, almost bald-headed feller with a bushy beard, and he had crinkly blue eyes that laughed when he talked. He looked for all the world like the cowboy Gabby Hayes.

"Will you read my palm for me?" Billy said to Cassie.

"I will for shore!" she said. "I wanna hear 'In the Pines.'"

"All right, then!" I heard a woman's voice there beside Billy. "Toss down my mandolin, honey chile, and hand me my rum, Billy Blue."

"Your rum?" Billy said. "Now, Bonnie Blue, didn't you promise me you'd never drink another drop?"

"Heck no, Billy! I promised never to drop another drink! So hand it to me careful."

We laughed louder and longer than the joke was worth, 'cause we knew it was only part of their act, and Bonnie was not really going to drink rum.

The other two Blues women, who were introduced as Nancy Lou Blue and Nancy Too Blue, got up in the aisle to retrieve their instruments. There was no telling how old anybody was in this group. They all had on bright colors, lots of fringe, rhinestones, and cowboy boots and hats. I suspected the women were wearing wigs, 'cause nobody could naturally have that much blond hair.

Bonnie Blue said to Cassie, "Who you got there wid'ja?"

"This is Gypsy and Woodrow," Cassie introduced us.

We said hey, then Cassie said to us, "Let's give the band our seat so they can spread out and have room for all their stuff."

It was agreed, and with much bustle and jostling, we changed places with Billy and Bonnie. The two Nancys joined them.

Billy played the guitar, Bonnie the mandolin, Nancy Lou the banjo, and Nancy Too the fiddle. They were fooling around with the strings to get tuned up, and I settled between Woodrow and Cassie. The three of us were on our knees looking back.

"Are they all in the same family?" I asked Cassie.

"Naw, they're not even related," Cassie said. "They take the name of Blue when they're performing."

Suddenly the band cut loose with "In the Pines" as pretty as you please, and their music just filled me up. We started keeping time by clapping, and in some places where we knew the words, we sang along. The Luckys, who now occupied the seat where the two Nancys had been, imitated every move we made. Their faces were shining. The other passengers patted their feet and craned their necks to see the band.

Then pretty Ruby started dancing in the aisle up near the front, and she could dance good. In a minute Tootsie started dancing with her.

The first song ended, and everybody whooped and clapped.

"'Bury Me Beneath the Willow'!" came a holler. "You know that one?"

"Do de queen speak English?" Billy said.

And off they went into "Bury Me Beneath the Willow," followed by "I'm So Lonesome I Could Cry," and a man got up and danced slow with Tootsie, while Ruby sat down and sang along with the band. She had a sweet voice.

When they were finished with that one, Nancy Lou said, "'Blue Eyes Crying in the Rain.' Everybody knows that one."

That song was a real tearjerker, and we crooned pitifully, milking it for all it was worth. When it was over, Woodrow said, "Now do something jolly."

"Okay, just one more," Billy Blue said. "We have to rest up for Deep Vale."

Then the band twanged a lively rendition of "Ain't We Crazy?" Ruby got up and danced again, and the young man named Chester danced with her. After that we gave the Bluegrass Blues a huge round of applause and helped them put their instruments away again.

We could hear Cassie murmuring behind us as she read Billy Blue's palm.

Woodrow whispered to me, "Running into the band was another sign."

"How do you figure that?" I said.

"I dunno why exactly," he said. "But we keep coming across the word *blue*. There's the name of the band, Bluegrass Blues, and their last name is Blue, and they play bluegrass music. They played 'Blue Eyes Crying in the Rain' while we were coming home from Bluefield!"

I didn't say anything, but I figured that was stretching it a bit. You could run this sign thing into the ground.

"The first midget we ever saw had on a blue dress!" he went on excitedly. "And the Lucky girls have blue flowers on *their* dresses."

"Don't forget the sky," I said sarcastically. "It was blue until we got to *Blue*field."

Woodrow looked at me doubtfully and said no more about signs.

The band left us in Deep Vale, and we reclaimed our seat. As we left that town, our mood began to list toward the dark side. We were in total blackness because Pap did not turn the inside lights on for us this time. The temperature had dropped considerable, and in the headlights you could see the sleet coming down fast and thick, making sharp pinging sounds as the pellets hit the windows.

When we started up the mountain toward Lucky Ridge, where the Luckys would be getting off the bus, I thought of those steep drop-offs over the edge of the road. In the dark you couldn't see the bottom of the deep hollows below. You could see nothing but this big, yawning murkiness over there. I shivered.

The Luckys snuck back in the dark to eavesdrop on us, but there was nothing to hear. So they snuggled together at one end of our wide seat.

The rhythm of the wheels had almost lulled me to sleep when I heard Woodrow say to the kids, "Where do y'all live?"

"Right now we're stayin' wid Granddaddy in the Lucky Ridge Coal Camp," the boy said.

"What were you doin' in Bluefield?"

"Went to see our daddy," one of the girls said.

"Your daddy? Don't he live with y'all?"

"He's in the jailhouse," the other girl said.

"What for?"

"Moonshinin'," the boy said. "He was just trying to give us young'uns some Christmas. But they throwed him in jail, and now we're on relief."

Lucky Ridge was the coal camp I had seen that morning. That seemed like such a long time ago. What an awful place to have to go home to! I snuggled deeper into my seat and thought of Mama and Porter waiting for me in our cozy, sheltered ranch house on Residence Street. And it occurred to me that Lucky should be *my* name.

"I got me a dawg," the Lucky boy said. "He's a good old coon dawg."

"What's his name?" Woodrow said drowsily.

"Blue."

1 2 ◄

When I got home, Mama had supper ready, but I was almost too tired to eat. I managed to swallow a few bites between sentences as I told her and Porter about Joseph and Miz Lincoln. Then I stumbled off to bed, tossed my dirty clothes into a pile on the floor, wrapped myself in a clean flannel nightgown, and crawled between crisp sheets. I was asleep in a jiffy.

Mama did not make me get up and go to church the next morning. I couldn't remember the last time that had happened, and it felt good to sleep in. When I heard her and Porter go out the front door, I turned over and listened to the rain spattering against my window.

I couldn't sleep anymore, but I wasn't ready to get up. I lifted the curtain and peeped out at the gray weeping world and the dripping orchard. It was hard to imagine spring, when the apple trees would be all decked out in their white lace.

I turned on my radio, which had been a Christmas present from Porter. Most of the stations had nothing but preaching on Sunday morning, but there was this one station out of Richlands that played the latest music all the time, and told good jokes, too. So that's where I turned the dial. Kitty Wells's voice filled my room, and I sank again into the pillows.

My mind went to all the people I had been with yesterday. It seemed sad and strange to me that so many of them had lost one or both parents. Miz Lincoln's parents had given her away like she was a puppy or a kitten. Then her adopted parents had died. Cassie's mama and grandma had both died. The Luckys' daddy was in jail. Joseph's daddy had abandoned him. And my own daddy? He had taken his own life.

Then, of course, there was Woodrow's mama. I had actually seen Aunt Belle only a few times in my life, but through Woodrow I felt that I knew her well. Who woulda thought she could ever abandon him? The idea must seem even more incredible to him, and that was why it was so hard for him to let go.

I felt sure she had loved him with all her heart. They had made plans to get Woodrow's crossed eyes fixed. They had shared special moments together. Aunt Belle believed Woodrow had visited her from a far-off place in the moment before he was born. How could she possibly have left him?

Then I set aside my thoughts to listen to a joke on the radio. Oh yeah, this was a good one. I found a piece of paper and a pencil in my nightstand drawer and wrote it down before I could forget it.

After a while I managed to drag myself out of bed and fix a bowl of cornflakes. The house seemed awful cold and empty without Mama and Porter. I chucked some wood on the coals smoldering in the grate, and before long I had me a big old fire.

Mama and Porter found me all curled up on the couch in front of the fireplace, reading Nancy Drew, when they got home from church. It was all that I had promised myself yesterday during the cold rain in Bluefield.

Mama went straightaway to fix us some lunch, and Porter settled down with the Sunday edition of the *Bluefield Daily Telegraph*.

"I reckon Woodrow is becoming quite the traveler," Porter said to me.

"Whadda ya mean?" I said.

"Yesterday Bluefield, today Roanoke."

I sat up and looked at Porter. "Ro'noke?"

"Yeah, his Aunt Millie and Uncle Russell took him there today."

"His Aunt Millie and Uncle Russell?" I said. "What for?"

"To see his daddy."

"His daddy?"

"Is there an echo in here?" Porter said with a grin.

Porter relished any opportunity to tell folks interesting things they didn't already know. That's why the newspaper business fit him like a glove.

"Tell me!" I said.

"While you young'uns were galavantin' all over West Virginia, your grandpa had a long-distance call from Woodrow's daddy. He said he has admitted himself to a special hospital in Roanoke. His brother, Russell, and Russell's wife, Millie, were driving out there today to visit him, and he wanted Woodrow to come along."

"What's he in the hospital for?"

"To get dried out."

"What does that mean—to get dried out?"

"It means he's soggy with alcohol."

"In other words, he's an alcoholic," Mama said, coming in from the kitchen, "and he needs medical attention. Lunch is ready."

You didn't have to tell me and Porter twice to come and eat. We settled around the kitchen table, said the blessing, and began to fill our plates.

"Does that mean Uncle Everett is addicted to alcohol?" I asked.

"Yes, alcoholism is an addiction," Mama said.

"That's another thing Woodrow and Joseph have in common," I said. "Joseph's daddy is addicted to gambling. Is there a hospital for that, too?"

"I don't know," Porter said, "but there should be."

"How long will Uncle Everett be there?"

"He'll probably be hospitalized for a month or so, but he plans to stay in Roanoke permanently," Porter said.

"He's moving away from Crooked Ridge?" I asked.

"Yeah, he has a job offer in Roanoke, if he straightens himself out. He also wants to stay near the hospital in case he backslides."

"Do you think he'll make Woodrow move with him?"

"No, I don't think so," Mama said. "You see, Gypsy, there's a woman in the picture now, and it's my bet she does not want Woodrow."

"You mean Woodrow's daddy is gonna get married again?"

"I think so," Mama went on. "Everett wants to file for a divorce from Belle. That's another thing he said on the phone."

"Does Woodrow know that?"

"He'll find out today," Mama said with a sigh. "Poor kid."

"How could Uncle Everett do that to Aunt Belle when she's not even here to speak for herself?"

"I doubt seriously that she would care if she were here," Porter said.

"I think she'd be glad," Mama agreed. "But it's still hard on Woodrow. They're his parents, and he loves them both."

I told Mama and Porter more details about our trip. I talked about Cassie and Pap, the old toothless man, the Bluegrass Blues, and the Luckys. But they were most interested in Joseph and Miz Lincoln.

"How tall would you say she is?" Mama wanted to know.

"She'd come about up to my shoulder," I said.

"Is that right?" Mama said. Her eyes were big. "I wonder how she goes about shopping for clothes? Does she shop in the children's department, or what?"

Porter laughed. "You would think of that."

As the day wore on, Mama let me be as lazy as I wanted to be, and between naps I finished my Nancy Drew mystery. A person needs a day like this once in a while, I thought. Life with Woodrow had turned into one never-ending adventure, and that can wear you out.

When Woodrow came home, late that evening, he did not tramp across the yard to see me, like I thought he would. I was surprised, but I pulled myself off the couch and ran next door through the mud puddles to find out what was happening. I was even more surprised when I got there and learned that Woodrow was already in bed.

Granny and Grandpa were sitting on the couch, watching *The Ed Sullivan Show*. I settled down between them, and Dawg squirmed right under my feet. I petted her.

"I think Woodrow's a little depressed," Granny said. "Even when you have a rough childhood as he did, it's hard to say goodbye to it."

"Did he tell y'all what happened today?" I asked.

"Yeah," Grandpa said. "His daddy told him that a relative is planning to move into their house on Crooked Ridge. He told Woodrow to go there and look through his mother's things, decide what he wants to keep, and dispose of the rest. He talked about Belle as if she were dead."

"So when are you gonna take Woodrow up there to Crooked Ridge?" I said.

"It has to be this Saturday," Grandpa said. "The feller wants to move in the following week."

"Woodrow was planning to go back to Bluefield on Saturday," I said.

Grandpa shrugged. "He can't do both."

The next morning the rain had stopped, and I met Woodrow, as usual, to walk to school. He was quiet, and I didn't push it. He would tell me everything by and by.

When we got to Mr. Collins's homeroom, Cassie came rushing up to us, grabbed Woodrow's arm with one hand and mine with the other, and pulled us off into a private corner away from our classmates.

"What was in the letter?" she whispered excitedly to Woodrow.

"What letter?" he said.

"The letter your mama wrote to you. I know she did! I dreamed it."

"I didn't get it!" Woodrow said, and now he was excited, too. "Maybe it will come today!"

"No, no, no!" Cassie said. "She wrote it before she left you. In the dream she was standing on a stairway with a letter in her hand. There was one word on the envelope, wrote out in large block letters—WOODROW."

"How do you know it was before she left?"

"Because she was sad to be leaving you. She was crying!"

Woodrow was stunned into silence.

"So there wadn't no letter from her to you?" Cassie prodded.

"No, me and Daddy and the sheriff and everybody searched the cabin good. We looked ever'where for any clues. If there'd been a letter, we'd a' found it."

"It's another parallel to Joseph's story," I whispered. "His daddy sent him a letter that he never got, and your mama wrote you a letter that you never got."

"That's right!" Woodrow said. "Read the signs!" He turned to Cassie again. "In the dream, what was Mama wearing?"

"I couldn't see that," Cassie said. "She was standing in the shadows."

"On a stairway?" Woodrow said. "There's no stairs

there in the cabin. There's a ladder going up to the loft, that's all."

"Maybe that was it," Cassie said.

"Saturday me and Gypsy are going up there to my old house," Woodrow said.

It was the first time I had heard I was going along, but that was okay. Me and Woodrow assumed a lot of things about each other these days.

"Go with us, Cassie!" he went on. "Maybe you'll pick up something while you're there."

"What about Bluefield?" Cassie said.

"Bluefield will have to wait. Daddy's cousin Calvin is gonna move into the house next week, and I've gotta sift through Mama's things."

"Sure, I'd like to go," Cassie said. "Pap can get by without me one Saturday."

Bitter cold days followed, but the sky was clear. I had a new wool hat to keep my ears warm, but I soon decided I must have an allergy to wool, because it made my head itch something awful. On Thursday morning, as Woodrow and I walked to school, I had to stop for a moment, and ask him to hold my books while I took off the hat to scratch my head.

He stood there without a word, watching me scratch. It appeared that his mind was anywhere but in the moment, or he would have been laughing at me. Since the weekend he had grown more and more gloomy, which was definitely not his nature, and he had dived into his schoolwork like he was consumed with it. He studied every hour he was not sleeping or eating or doing his chores.

"I haven't seen you without your nose in a book this whole week," I said.

He didn't answer. I replaced the hat and tied the string under my chin. I took my books from him, and we continued our walk.

"You know what they say about all work and no play," I chided him. "What's it gonna get'cha to study so hard, anyhow?"

"It'll get me to be the smartest person in the world," he answered in all seriousness. "I'm gonna read Grandpa's whole set of encyclopedias."

"What!"

"That's right. I started on Monday, and I won't be doing anything for fun till I've finished."

"How far are you up to now?"

"I am up to *aardvark*."

I 3 ◄

On Saturday morning the radio weatherman predicted snow for the afternoon, so Grandpa was uneasy in his mind about starting up an isolated holler like Crooked Ridge without chains on the tires of his new car. By the time he'd drug the chains out of his storage shed, and Porter helped him put them on over the tires, it was close to eleven and the snow clouds were hovering.

Mama was down at the church house doing something or other, and Cassie had been with me since nine o'clock, waiting. We were both wearing our jeans that day, as well as heavy sweaters and boots. While we waited for Grandpa, I picked out a few songs on the piano that the Bluegrass Blues had done for us. I thought I did a pretty good job playing, but when Cassie and I tried to sing like Bonnie and the two Nancys, it was plain even to us that we should never try to make a living at it.

Woodrow couldn't wait to get started. He wandered

in and then out of our house, restless but quiet. He was still in a dark mood, which surprised me. Normally, Woodrow did not stay down in the mouth for long.

Finally, Porter came in, stopped in the kitchen to wash his hands, and yelled to me and Cassie, "Okay, girls, Grandpa and Woodrow are ready and waiting for you."

Cassie and I grabbed our coats, scarves, gloves, and hats and hurried out the door. Woodrow had laid down on the horn before we got to the car.

"Git a move on!" he hollered.

He was sitting in the front seat with Grandpa, so me and Cassie climbed into the rear.

"All right, you girls, listen up," Grandpa said. "If road conditions get too bad up there at Crooked Ridge, we're not gonna try to drive home in the dark. We'll have to spend the night. Are y'all ready to do that?"

"You mean sleep in that place?" I said.

Over the top of the seat, Woodrow shot me the dirtiest look he had.

"I slept there for twelve years!" he said hotly. "I don't reckon one night is gonna spoil your pretty looks!"

"I didn't mean it like that," I protested weakly.

"Porter said if we're not home by dark, he'll call the bus station and leave a message there for your daddy," Grandpa said to Cassie. "Is that gonna be all right?"

"Yeah," Cassie said.

"Are you sure?" Grandpa persisted.

"I'm sure," Cassie said. "Pap won't worry about me as long as he knows what's going on, and that I'm with y'all."

"Is there anything up there to eat, Woodrow?" I said, because I was already hungry for lunch.

Woodrow didn't answer, and I knew right then I had ruffled his feathers good.

"Granny fixed us a big old picnic basket full of stuff," Grandpa said quickly. "It's in the trunk. So, is everybody with us?"

"Yes," Cassie and I said together.

I wanted to run into the house for my toothbrush and nightgown, but seeing the mood Woodrow was in, I didn't dare.

As we hit the highway and picked up speed, the tire chains made quite a racket. Above the noise, Cassie and I kept up a constant stream of chatter. We were excited about driving to such an out-of-the-way place with a possible snowstorm coming. It was another adventure with Woodrow. But he rode all the way to the mouth of Crooked Ridge wordless and motionless, except for scratching his head a bit.

Once we got there, he said, "This is where you turn, Grandpa."

"I know, I know," Grandpa said. "I'm not senile yet, boy."

The holler curled up and up between the mountains,

becoming more and more narrow and rocky as we went. I wondered what would happen if we were to meet a coal truck, because there was not room for even two cars to pass, much less a truck. But we didn't meet any- body, so I didn't find out. A light snow started, and Grandpa had to turn on his windshield wipers. Suddenly he pulled over to one side of the road and stopped the car. We were in front of the Prater house.

I had not been here many times in my life, and the last time was maybe two years before Aunt Belle disap- peared. I had nearabout forgot how desolate and run- down the place was. It was a sorry sight.

A wisp of a memory came to me then. In the summer sun I saw me and Woodrow as little bitty kids, no more'n three or four, playing in the creek there behind the house while Mama and Aunt Belle picked blackber- ries on the bank. It was one of the few times Mama had taken me to see them, and it had been a right nice day.

I recalled the water sparkling in the sunshine, and me and Woodrow trying to catch the glitter in our hands. The pebbles were round and firm under our baby toes.

Returning to the present moment, I saw that the sea- sons had turned it into a different place. For one thing, the creek was froze around the edges, and you'd have to be crazy to stick your toes in there. Also, the gray hills, towering steep and rugged all around us, showed no trace of that long-ago summer's green.

The snow was coming down harder. When we got out of Grandpa's car, I was struck by the quiet. We coulda been the last people living in the world.

Woodrow's face took on no particular expression, but I saw him swallow hard. It was the first time he had returned to this place where he had spent his childhood with his mama.

"I'll start a fire," Grandpa said lightheartedly, and slapped Woodrow's shoulder playfully, trying to cheer him up, I reckoned. "You think there's any firewood in there?"

Woodrow didn't answer. He stepped up on the low porch, and the rest of us followed. He gave the door a push, and it kinda fell open. One of the hinges was barely there. I could remember nothing about the interior of the cabin, and I wondered if I had ever been inside.

"It ain't changed a lot," Woodrow said, as he gazed into the darkness.

I peeped in but couldn't see much. The room was in shadows. Hesitantly, we went inside. I could see a window at each end of the room, but they did not give much light. Automatically, I reached for a light switch, but there was none.

"Where's the light switch?" I asked Woodrow.

He walked to the center of the room and yanked a cord, but nothing happened.

"I shoulda knowed it," he said sourly. "Daddy didn't pay the juice bill."

I shivered. I hadn't counted on spending the day—and possibly the night—in a place with no electricity. After all, this was the middle of the twentieth century!

"Got any lanterns?" Grandpa said.

"There may be one up in the loft," Woodrow said.

When my eyes were adjusted to the dimness, I could see a big stone fireplace along the wall by the front door, a ratty couch before it, two armchairs, and various other pieces of worn-out furniture. It was a dismal, melancholy room.

On the end wall to our left was a coal cookstove, and behind it the wall was papered with pages from a Sears and Roebuck catalog. There were two tall gray porcelain cabinets for dishes and things, and a wooden table with four chairs. Near it was a washstand that held a water bucket, a dipper, and a wash pan. A dirty green towel was hanging from a rack on the side of it.

On the wall facing us as we went in, there was a doorway that led into the one bedroom. Right beside it was a homemade ladder that went into the loft. I looked up there and saw a gate at the top of the ladder. The loft had never been finished proper, and it was more like a balcony than a real room. It had a plank fence across the front of it. I knew Woodrow had slept up there.

At that moment Woodrow was climbing up the ladder

in search of a lantern. I watched him open the gate onto a braided rug covering a plain board floor. The loft was tiny, barely deep enough for a straw-tick mattress against the wall, and a small chifforobe at the end, where Woodrow had no doubt kept his belongings.

Tucked into the roof, where it slanted over the bed, there was a small round window like ones I had seen on ships in the movies. It was the one touch of charm in this bleak place.

Woodrow climbed down the ladder with a kerosene lamp dangling from his arm. He carried it to one of the cabinets, fumbled around in a drawer for matches, lit the lamp, and set it on the table. The room's dark shadows melted.

"There orta be enough firewood here to start with," Woodrow said, and pointed to a large covered box beside the fireplace. "And some kindlin' and paper."

Cassie and I huddled together on the couch while Grandpa and Woodrow got a blazing fire roaring up the chimney. The room took on a more friendly atmosphere right away. We got out of our overcoats, gloves, and hats, and studied the room.

You could imagine it was much nicer when Aunt Belle was here to take care of it. There were pictures hanging on the walls, alongside homemade crafts, probably created by Aunt Belle. Some of Woodrow's early childhood art was tacked to a board across the top of the bedroom door. We went in there and found a heating stove. It was more cheerful than the main room.

"Here's some slack coal," Grandpa said, peeping into a coal bucket by the stove. "I'll get us a fire started in here, too."

Woodrow removed some well-worn quilts and pillows from a wardrobe, carried them out into the main room, and spread them on the floor in front of the fireplace.

"This is where I usta do my homework," he said, and plopped himself down.

"Like old Abe Lincoln himself," I commented.

It was just something to say, but once again Woodrow bristled and stabbed me with an icy glare. Was he going to take everything as an insult?

"Well, you see how old Abe turned out," Cassie said brightly, trying to lighten him up.

Grandpa found a screwdriver and fixed the hinge on the front door so that it closed and opened proper. After that, he drew up a bucket of water from the well outside, and Woodrow hauled in the picnic basket.

"I guess we better go out and fetch some more firewood, Woodrow," Grandpa said. "This here won't last long."

So the two of them went up on the hillside into the woods, which by that time were covered with a powdery snow, and Cassie and I set about making a picnic lunch on the kitchen table. Granny had fixed fried chicken, biscuits, potato salad, green beans, apple fritters, and iced tea in a jug. It was enough food for ten people.

We found plates, glasses, and forks in the cabinets, but no napkins.

"I'm not gonna ask Woodrow if there's napkins," I said. "He's liable to knock my head off."

Cassie chuckled.

If Woodrow didn't change his ways, I thought, he would be the subject of my next New Year's Revelation. I could see myself standing up in front of the family in the living room, saying, "The thing I want to get off my chest is about Woodrow. No matter who or what he's mad at, he takes it out on me, and I'm sick and tired of it!"

That would fix him. I wondered if I could wait a whole year.

The snow was coming down fast and furious, and it took Woodrow and Grandpa an hour to find enough firewood. Most of it they piled in and around the woodbox, and the rest they stacked on the front porch. Only then were they ready to eat. Cassie and I were drooling by that time.

We gathered at the table, said the blessing, and filled our plates. Then we settled on the quilts before the fire, which crackled and flickered, making the room seem almost cheerful.

It was going to be quite the storm. You couldn't call it

a blizzard, because we didn't have such things in our part of the country, but the wind had picked up considerable. I could hear it shooshing around the corners of the cabin, and I walked to one of the windows to look out at the wild white flurries.

I could barely make out the road, which wound up between the hills like a clean, white ribbon. There were no tire tracks on it, and I realized that we had not heard a vehicle going up or down the holler since we got here. Yeah, this was a desolate place all right, and it was going to be a long night if we had to stay, which was a real possibility.

I sat down again and stole a peek at Grandpa and Woodrow, who appeared unconcerned. Woodrow seemed like a small replica of Grandpa as they shoveled in their food, washed it down with tea, and wiped their mouths on their shirtsleeves, almost in unison. To a stranger Woodrow coulda passed for Grandpa's own boy.

In the 1890s Grandpa had been a boy his own self, growing up on the top of Wiley Mountain, which was about as far out in the sticks as you could get. He had an old-timey, backwoods upbringing, but he always talked about it with warm looks on his face, like he'd go back if he could. So this was a return to childhood for him.

Right then Grandpa said, "Listen to that wind!" He grinned. "That's a real snowstorm out there."

Woodrow smiled in spite of himself. A person has to

work hard at staying in a lousy mood when he's having such a good time, I thought.

Drek'ly, Grandpa set his plate aside, rubbed his belly, and belched. Woodrow did the same. I figured if they'd had cigars, they'd a' lit 'em up right then and there, and settled back for a contented smoke, like Grandpa sometimes did at home.

Yeah, they were both in their element. That was it. They were roughing it like the old-timers did, and they didn't have to worry about good manners or appearances or anything else.

I nudged Cassie and said, "Let's go to the bathroom."

At which Woodrow exploded with laughter.

"Bathroom!" he managed to splutter.

Grandpa started laughing, too.

Cassie and I rolled our eyes at each other as we bundled up in our heavy gear again. We knew there was not really a bathroom. It was simply an outhouse there by the creek. I had been in people's houses before who didn't have bathrooms, so it was not my first time, for crying out loud. And Cassie Caulborne had been raised in a place almost like Crooked Ridge, so she had used outhouses most of her life. Then what was so funny?

"Don't forget to flush!" Woodrow hollered as we went out the door, and we could hear them laughing until the wind drowned them out.

I 4 ◄

I took Cassie's hand as we stepped into the storm and started toward the toilet by the creek, which was a short piece from the rear of the house. Snow lodged in my eyelashes and blinded me. To keep my bearings, I moved along the side of the building.

Unexpectedly, as we rounded a corner, the snow simply quit and the wind went away mysteriously to another place, where I could hear its distant echo as in a well. The air grew thick and warm, and a hundred voices whispered in whirling vapors around my head.

Talk about fey! I stopped in my tracks, and Cassie moved close in beside me.

"What in the world . . . ?" she said.

We clutched each other as the thing rolled over us again, and brought me a memory with it.

Almost a year ago Woodrow had told me about this place behind his house, where the air was thick and vibrating. He had said when you hit this warm spot, you could feel the air quivering, and you could hear noises. I had asked him what kind of noises, and he had said they were voices—funny voices.

So this was it! The place where the two worlds touch! Later on, he had told me it wasn't real. He said him and his mama had made it up. But here it was. It felt real to me.

The whispers softened. You could not understand the words, but I thought I could feel puffs of breath on my cheeks and a pulsing of warm air. I trembled. And then it was gone. Once again the cold wind was pushing down my coat collar and the snow was blinding me.

Cassie and I hurried on to the outhouse.

By the time we returned, Grandpa had hung a pot of water on a hook over the fire to heat, for washing dishes. Woodrow was no place to be seen, so I figured he was in the bedroom, going through his mama's things. I went in there.

"Woodrow," I said. "I found the hole in the air you told me about."

"Huh?" he said, lifting his eyes from a cigar box full of papers and photographs.

"You know, the place where the two worlds touch. I felt it! Cassie did, too."

"Oh, that," Woodrow said, unimpressed. "Aunt Millie said it was some kind of natural phenomena having to do with the air currents coming down the holler between the hills."

"But you told me——" I tried to protest.

"Yeah, I know, I told you a lot of stuff," he said irritably. "Something's there all right. You can feel it. But it ain't no place where the two worlds touch. Me and Mama made that up to entertain ourselves. I told you we made it up!"

He turned again to his chore like he was dismissing the whole subject, and me with it.

"You usta think your mama was in that place," I said, hoping he would talk to me and not be so mad.

But my words had the opposite effect. He slammed the cigar box on the floor.

"That's stupid, Gypsy," he yelled at me. "You just don't get it, do you? I told you what happened. She dressed up in my clothes and snuck out of here. My daddy said she left him and she left me on purpose, 'cause she didn't love us anymore. And he's right. Case closed!"

He continued to glare at me. I was vaguely aware of Grandpa and Cassie at the bedroom door, watching and listening, but I didn't care. Now I was mad, too.

"Well, I don't believe it!" I yelled back at him. "I know Aunt Belle loved you and would never do such a thing! I don't believe she'd just abandon you, and if you do, then you . . . you're . . ."

I couldn't think of what it was I wanted to say.

He crossed his arms and peered over his glasses at me. "I'm what?"

"I don't know," I finished lamely. "But I liked you lots better when you hoped for the best."

"Well, I don't hope for anything now," he said bitterly. "Why should I?"

I could sense his tears just below the surface.

"I don't know, Woodrow, but *I* still do."

I charged past Grandpa and Cassie, into the main room, and found some soap flakes for washing dishes. Cassie, tying one of Aunt Belle's aprons around her waist, came up beside me.

"I found this hanging on a nail behind the bedroom door," she said quietly. "Maybe if I wear something that belonged to her, I'll get a feel for her."

We commenced cleaning up the kitchen area in silence. Later Cassie and I settled down in front of the fireplace again, while Grandpa sat near us and started whittling on a chunk of wood with his pocketknife. Woodrow stayed in the bedroom, poring over his mama's belongings.

There was no talk at all about driving home. No doubt Grandpa and Woodrow had hoped to spend the night all along. Woodrow had left his new watch at home, and nobody else was wearing one, so we had no idea what time it was. We did know that dark crept over us much earlier than usual.

At suppertime we finished off the picnic food, and it was a'plenty. Woodrow ate in silence and stared into the flames, which threw dancing shadows into the far corners of the room.

"Don't be blue, son," Grandpa said kindly, placing an arm across Woodrow's shoulders.

"Blue?" Woodrow said, raising his eyes to Grandpa. "Why'd you use that word?"

Grandpa shrugged. "It's a good word."

Woodrow glanced at me, then continued studying the fire.

"I'm whooped," Grandpa said a while later. "I been up since five-thirty, and it's time for old men like me to turn in."

It was decided that Grandpa and Woodrow would take the bedroom, and Cassie and I could sleep in the loft.

"Now, you young'uns don't stay up too late, you heah me?" Grandpa said as he went off to bed.

We said good night, and Woodrow lighted Grandpa's way to bed with the lantern. Then he brought it again into the main room and sat with me and Cassie on the quilts.

"Hey, let me read y'all's palms now," Cassie said. "You first, Woodrow. Let's see what we can see."

Woodrow silently stuck out his hand, palm up, for Cassie. She studied it for some time, traced the lines with her index finger, nodded her head slowly like some wise old professor, and mumbled things to herself.

"Uh-huh . . . ah, I see . . . That's not so clear . . . but oh, yes, this is good . . ." Finally she began her reading. "The Mount of Mars shows me that you have great vitality and courage. On the Mount of Luna I can see travel lines that indicate you are going to far places. The Life line is deep and long, yes, very long."

They sounded like somebody else's words, but Woodrow stayed perfectly still and listened close.

Then Cassie went into a fast spin, stringing sentences together almost like she was reading out loud in class, painting a muddled, fuzzy picture of Woodrow's future accomplishments in school, job, and family. I don't like to say it, but it sounded put on to me.

When she seemed to be done, he said, "And what else?"

"Not much," she confessed.

"What about Mama?" he said.

"I can't see anything about her."

Cassie went through the same list of *ah*s and *uh-huh*s for me that she had for Woodrow. Then she began. She told me pretty near the same thing she had told him. I was wondering if everybody got the same reading from her, when suddenly she paused over a funny wee dimple near the beginning of my Life line. She touched it, and her face took on an expression of pity.

"Oh, Gypsy, this is sad," she said.

"What is it?" I said, alarmed at her tone.

"When you were a real little girl . . ."

I jerked my hand away from her, feeling like she'd been reading my diary. Was it possible that Cassie had somehow tapped into the most dreadful event of my life?

"I didn't see it all," Cassie said.

"Somebody told you," I said, glancing at Woodrow.

"Nobody told me," she said. "But I'd like to know."

I began massaging the palm of my hand as if the pain were there. I wondered if my wound had healed enough so that I could talk about it now. Maybe I could tell Cassie. She was plainly interested. People were naturally curious about things like this.

"My daddy took his own life," I said matter-of-factly. Then, turning to the fire, I added with more feeling, "How could a person do that, I wonder?"

It was not a question you could answer, and we sat without speaking for what seemed like a long, long time. We could hear Grandpa snoring, but nobody laughed. The shadows on the walls no longer danced with the same energy. They seemed tired and hazy.

After a while Woodrow stood up and began to poke at the fire with the poker. Then he walked to a cabinet and pulled out a fruit jar full of popcorn kernels. Next he took an iron skillet from a peg above the cookstove, slapped a big dollop of lard into it, and set it into the hot coals at the edge of the fire. When the lard was melted, Woodrow threw salt into it, then about half a cup of the popcorn. He placed a cover over the skillet, and we waited to hear the popping begin.

Finally, the corn began to pop, first at slow intervals, then faster. Now and again, Woodrow would shake the skillet to keep the popcorn from burning. At last, when the lid started rising off the skillet, he set it on the hearth, and we had the best popcorn I had ever tasted.

"Being here in the snow reminds me of a story," said Woodrow as we picked the popcorn hulls from our teeth with broom straws. "Wanna hear it?"

Of course we did.

"It's the truth," he went on. "It happened during the first snow of the winter. Matter o' fact, I think it was the *only* snow of that winter. But it wadn't no big one like this one. It was just enough to slick up the place.

"I was around eight or nine, I reckon, and I was spending the day with Uncle Russell 'cause Daddy was working, and Mama and Aunt Millie were gone to Richlands to see a doctor."

Woodrow stopped talking and stared thoughtfully into the fire.

"It was good to see Uncle Russell again the other day. I usta see him a lot, and I've missed him," he said.

Then he came back to the story.

"Uncle Russell had this horse that was old, sway-backed, and ornery as sin, but we were attached to that booger, both of us. His name was Thistle. That day Uncle Russell went to the barn and hooked him up to an empty sled. We were fixing to take him down the hill where there were some sacks of store-bought feed we needed to haul from the house, in the bottom, back to the barn, which was up the hill a piece.

"I'm not talking about a toy like you ride down the slope in the snow for fun. This contraption was about the size of the bed on a pickup truck. It was made of plain flat boards, and it had two runners, one on each side. It was just used for hauling stuff, with the horse pulling it.

"Well, like I said, it was slippery as butter out there, and me and Uncle Russell neither one had on boots. We didn't have any. The bottoms of our shoes were slick, and we were having quite the time just staying on our feet, much less guiding the horse.

"We got Thistle headed in the right direction, and Uncle Russell hollered at him to giddy-yap. Thistle started off down the path at a trot, and no matter how hard we pulled on the reins, we couldn't slow him down. Near-about all we could do was hold on tight, and try to follow without breaking our necks.

"Then all of a sudden, the runners picked up some speed, and got going faster than Thistle was going. First thing we knew, it had crashed into the horse's behind and knocked his legs out from under him. Wham! Down he went right on top of the boards with his legs just a'pawin' the air like he was running to heaven.

"That sled with the horse on top of it took off like a bullet, and picked up the momentum of a freight train! Me and Uncle Russell went running and falling, running and falling, and we couldn't keep up! Next thing we knew, horse and all had rounded the curve and gone out of sight down the road.

"We were total breathless as we reached the bend. There we saw old man Leslie Matney, who was about ninety, and he said to us, 'Lordy mercy, you ain't gonna believe what I saw just now—a horse ridin' a sled!'

"When we finally caught up with Thistle, we saw he had come to rest as pretty as you please against a bank. He was sitting there on the sled, looking around him, not hurt one bit.

"We like to laughed ourselves silly while we were hugging that horse and trying to help him up on his feet."

Me and Cassie laughed hard, too, and when Woodrow would repeat parts of it, we'd get to laughing again, harder than before. When we were all the way laughed out, Woodrow went to the window.

"The snow's stopped," he said. "As a matter of fact, I think I can see a few stars."

Cassie and I joined him at the window.

"Lookee, you can see the chim'ly smoke coming around the corner there where the two worlds touch. It don't know which way to go," said Woodrow.

We watched the smoke swirling one way, then another. I looked at the hills. It was really beautiful out there, but cold and remote. Once again, I felt isolated, like maybe the Russians had come over and blowed up the whole United States, except for us tucked away in this holler.

"It's lonely," I said.

"Yeah, and scary," Cassie said. "Can you imagine being out there in the night with no house to go to, and being cold and afraid, and alone in the dark?"

We thought about that for a moment, then Woodrow said, "What's the scariest place in the world?"

We sat on our quilts before the fire again, and thought some more.

The bottom of the ocean at midnight. Lost in a deep dark cave. A cemetery. Buried alive! Yeah, that was it. It was unanimous. Waking up in a casket buried alive had to be the scariest place in the world.

"That reminds me of something," Cassie said. "You know that old saying 'saved by the bell'?"

Yeah, we had heard it.

"Well, let me tell you how it got started. See, long time ago, they didn't use to embalm people. They just buried them, guts and all, when they quit breathing.

"Then one time when they had to move a graveyard, they found some skeletons that looked like they had been trying to get out of the grave. And the people felt bad that they had maybe buried some people alive.

"So after that, they started tying a string around the dead person's finger. It would lead up to the top of the ground where the other end was tied to a bell. So if the dead person woke up, he would pull the string and the bell would ring. That's why people say 'saved by the bell.'"

"That's interestin'," Woodrow said. "Did you read that in one of them history books?"

"No, I remember it. I was there."

"You were *there*?" Woodrow and I said together.

"Yeah . . . well, maybe I wasn't there as Cassie, and maybe I wasn't there in the flesh, but I remember it. It's a kind of ancestral memory that runs in my family."

Me and Woodrow gave each other our private "talk to you about this later" look, and I realized we were all the way back to being buddies again, and sharing moments like this that maybe nobody else would appreciate.

"Well, I have heard," Woodrow said, "that every story that's ever been told to us, and every book we've ever read, is still inside of us. And even though we don't know it's there, a little reminder can bring it to the surface again."

"And speaking of bells," I said, "I am reminded of a real good joke."

"Oh, goody!" Woodrow said, and moved closer to me.

"When the Hunchback of Notre Dame died," I started off, "the word went out that a new bell ringer was needed for the church tower. The first man to apply didn't have any arms.

"This priest they had in charge asked the man, 'How can you ring a bell without arms?'

" 'Come on and I'll show you,' said the man.

"So him and the priest went up into the tower. To show his skill in bell ringing, the armless man took a running-go-start and ran into the bell with his face, and the bell rang loud.

"'Well, all right, then,' said the priest. 'The job is yours.'

"But it so happened that on the very first day of his new job, that poor armless man took a flying run at the bell, missed it complete, fell down from the tower, and was killed dead.

"There was a crowd gathered around the dead body and someone said, 'Who is this man?'

"The priest came upon the scene and said, 'I don't know his name, but his face rings a bell.'

Cassie and Woodrow started to laugh, but I put out a hand to stop them. "Wait! Don't laugh yet. There's more.

"Several days later," I went on, "another man came to apply for the job as bell ringer, and he told the priest that he was the brother of the poor armless man who fell to his death. This man was clumsy, but he did have two arms.

"'Well, all right, then,' said the priest. 'You can have the job.'

"But, lo and behold, on the very first day of his job the poor man stumbled and, just like his brother, he fell from the tower to his death.

"Once again a crowd gathered around the dead body and someone said, 'Who is this man?'

"The priest, who had come up on the scene, said, 'I don't know his name, but he's a dead ringer for his brother.'"

Cassie laughed until every curl on her head bounced up and down. In fact, we all had the silly giggles bad. For once I was glad that Grandpa was hard of hearing, or we woulda woke him up for sure. But I knew in my heart that Grandpa wouldn't come out and fuss at us even if we did wake him. He always said he loved to hear kids laughing. That's how he was.

"Bells, bells, bells," Cassie was able to say at last, and she wiped a tear away from her cheek.

"That's right," Woodrow said, "Belle, Belle, Belle. Her name just keeps on coming up. I wonder where she is tonight. Is she safe and warm?"

There was quiet again as we pondered Woodrow's words. The dark and cold combined to make us shiver, grateful to be inside the cabin. We were all lost in our own thoughts, and the air was thick with unanswered questions.

16

It had to be near midnight when we finally decided it was time to turn in.

"I wish I'd brought my nightgown," I said as Cassie and I started to climb the ladder to the loft.

"You're better off sleeping in your clothes," Woodrow advised.

"There's plenty of covers on the bed, ain't they?" Cassie said.

"Yeah, but it's still cold up there," said Woodrow. "You can take your boots off, but keep your socks on."

So we climbed into the loft and closed the gate. Woodrow was right. It was freezing up there. You could feel cold air coming through the cracks in the wall. Me and Cassie tugged each other's boots off and quickly slipped under the covers with our clothes on. We lay on our backs and scrunched up close to each other for warmth.

We could hear Woodrow banking the fire; then he called good night, dimmed the lamp, and took it into the bedroom, closing the door behind him. The fire had burned down and threw very little light into the loft.

"You skeered, Gypsy?" Cassie whispered.

"Not much," I said. "Are you?"

"No, I just thought you might be."

I looked out at the night sky through the porthole in the slanted roof.

"I don't think it's gonna snow anymore," I whispered. "The stars are really coming out now."

But Cassie was asleep. I snuggled deeper into the quilts and watched the night sky through the tiny window, until my eyes slowly closed.

We're far away, I was thinking, as I drifted off . . . far away from everybody . . . in the dark . . . in a loft . . . in a cabin . . . in the snow . . . in the hills . . . in the place . . . where . . .

I am dreaming of the place where the two worlds touch. I am falling in and swirling round and round and down through dim lights and muted voices. And everything is in slow motion. I am thinking what a slowed-down world this is, how cloudy and dull it all seems, when I see Aunt Belle just ahead. She is shining through the haze like a brilliant star.

Then came a piercing scream.

"She's on the ladder!" It was Cassie. "She's there on the ladder!"

"What . . . ?" Still asleep, I jumped up and bumped my head on the low ceiling. Where was I anyhow?

The room was black as coal. I could barely make out the porthole in the roof, but it brought me to awareness of being in the cabin. Cassie was sitting up in bed, and I eased myself down beside her, rubbing my head.

"She's coming up the ladder!" she screamed again. "Look! Here she comes!"

I felt a jolt of panic then. There was so much agitation in her voice that I couldn't help feeling afraid. Was somebody on the ladder? I crawled in close to Cassie and put my arms around her.

"Who's on the ladder?" I whispered.

"Belle Prater!" Cassie continued with her ranting. "She's coming up the ladder!"

Then it dawned on me that Cassie was having a nightmare.

"Wake up!" I began to shake her. "You're dreaming!"

Suddenly I heard real noises on the ladder, and there was a dim light below the gate. Somebody *was* there!

"What'n the world's all the hollerin' for?"

Woodrow's head popped up over the gate. He threw the light across me and Cassie in the bed. Grandpa came right behind him.

Cassie put up her hand to ward off the light. "Whatsa matter?" she mumbled.

"You like to scared me to death!" I told Woodrow.

"And y'all like to scared us to death!" he shot back.

"We heard screaming," Grandpa said. The two of them peered over the gate. "What's going on, anyhow?"

"Cassie had a nightmare," I said.

"I did?" Cassie said, seeming totally bewildered. Then, "Oh yeah, I did. I remember. It was the same dream, Woodrow. She was here on the ladder. I don't mind saying she skeered me good. She was talking like them voices in that place out yonder—that hole in the air. But she had an envelope in her hand with your name on it."

"What? Who?" Grandpa wanted to know.

Woodrow lifted the lantern over the gate, set it on the floor, then unhooked the gate, and eased up the last few steps to sit on the floor beside our bed. Grandpa stayed on the ladder as Woodrow told him about Cassie's dreams.

"I'm serious, Woodrow," Cassie said. "I know there's a letter here for you somewhere."

"Well, what can I say?" Woodrow said. "We searched this place good for any clues the day she left, and there was nothing."

"Did you and your mama maybe have a secret hiding place?" I asked.

"No, not that I can recall," he said thoughtfully.

"Well, okay," Grandpa joined in, and laid a hand across Woodrow's shoulder. "Supposin' you put yourself in her place and you're going out the door that morning, and you want to leave a letter strictly for Woodrow that nobody else will find, where you gonna put it? Think about it."

Woodrow did think, and we were silent.

"Well," he said at last, "I think I'd put it somewhere up here."

"In the loft?" Cassie said.

We all glanced around us.

"She prob'ly wouldn't want to wake me," Woodrow went on, "so she'd slip it under the gate. But in that case I woulda seen it as soon as I woke up."

"Under the gate," Grandpa said thoughtfully, chin in hand.

All eyes went to the spot where the letter would have been if Aunt Belle had come up the ladder that morning and slipped it under the gate. I guess the same lightbulb went on in all our brains at the same time, and everybody made a dive for the edge of the rug. But it could not be moved. It was nailed down at each corner and along the sides, too. Woodrow tried to slip his hand underneath, but it was too snug to the floor.

"Okay," Grandpa said. "We may have to tear the rug apart. Is that all right with you, Woodrow?"

"Yeah, it's older than you are, Grandpa."

With that we all started tugging at the rug's edge, struggling to pull it loose from the nails, and little by little it yielded. Strings of braids tore loose from the rug and stuck to the nail heads. We ceased our struggle and Woodrow's hand shot under the rug again. This time his face went bright with triumph.

"I feel something!"

And he pulled out an envelope with one large word written in block letters on the front—WOODROW.

It was obvious to us what had happened. When Aunt Belle had hastily pushed the letter underneath the loft gate that morning, she had accidentally slipped it under the rug. It had been there ever since.

Woodrow tore the letter open, and Grandpa held the lantern for him to read by. You could see his eyes scanning the single page rapidly, before he handed it to Grandpa, with a puzzled expression on his face. Then Grandpa read the letter, and Cassie and I nosed right in there and read for ourselves. It was one strange letter, for sure, all the sentences being strung together, with no punctuation.

woodrow i dreamed it again i had wings she was flying over the mountain i will go and find her now dont tell your daddy dont you see i have to go now it is the only way i have to find a way out i must hurry now i am so scared go to your uncle russell today do not delay tell him and millie to take you to your grandpas house they will do it i promise i will send for you as soon as i find her go to *your grandpas and wait for me you are my heart and my life i remain your loving mother forever*

"She was really crazy," Woodrow whispered, and shivered in the raw morning chill. "Just look at this letter. It's nuts."

"She was overwhelmed with emotional problems," Grandpa said kindly, as he placed an arm around Woodrow. "I think she was having a nervous breakdown. She didn't understand what was happening to her, and she was afraid."

Woodrow read the letter through once more, but this time aloud. Then he read it to himself again, moving his lips as he mouthed each word. We watched his brow wrinkle up and his fingers clutch the paper until the knuckles turned white.

"I will send for you," he said out loud. "Wait for me."

"She went to find her own self," I said. "That's what she had to do."

I was remembering last summer, when Porter had said to me about Belle, *"She actually vanished, you see, many years ago, when she was about your age. Now she is out there trying to find herself again."*

17 ◄

As we left the cabin just before noon, Woodrow looked back only once at the home of his childhood. He was probably thinking he would never spend another night there. Then he turned his face frontward, with a set to his chin that I recognized as determination. He loaded a cardboard box full of his mother's things into the trunk of Grandpa's car, and we were gone.

There was not a lot of talk among us as we drove back to Coal Station. You couldn't drive a car all the way to Cassie's house, so we dropped her off at the end of the bridge that crossed the river. From there, she would have to walk only a short distance down the railroad tracks.

For breakfast we had polished off the popcorn and some peaches that Aunt Belle had canned, so by the time we arrived home we were just about famished. I followed Woodrow into Grandpa's house first, hoping Granny might have something delicious to eat. Of course she did.

Grandpa went directly to the kitchen table. Me and Woodrow greeted Dawg, then settled down with Grandpa. Dawg curled up under the table, waiting for scraps. Woodrow didn't bring out the letter from Aunt Belle right off, or even mention it. But I knew he would share it in his own good time.

Granny began to pull things out of her refrigerator just as Mama entered the back door with a flourish. Fresh from singing in the choir, she was dressed in an emerald green wool suit, her blue eyes sparkling. She looked for all the world like Doris Day. It occurred to me that Woodrow and I had missed church two Sundays in a row, and God had not struck us dead.

"Did you tell them?" Mama said to Granny.

"No, I'll let you tell them," Granny said, also smiling.

She had our attention.

Mama sat down at the kitchen table with us and said, "You will never guess who called!"

She waited for a guess, but we all sat there staring at her. Hunger had dulled our wits.

"Miz Lincoln!" Mama said.

We reacted quick enough to that.

"What'd she say?"

"She wanted to know if the snow had kept you from Bluefield yesterday, and she asked if you were coming next weekend. She has something to tell you."

"Did she say what it was?" Woodrow asked.

Granny set a platter of carrot sticks, celery, cukes, and radishes on the table.

"Yes," Mama said, and she made a big production of plucking a stick of celery from the platter, biting into it with a resounding crunch, and smiling triumphantly around the room.

"And?" I tried to hurry her along.

"She remembered seeing Belle."

"No foolin'?" Grandpa said. "Where?"

"It was last summer," Mama went on, "when the circus was in town. Miz Lincoln went to see some of her old friends and former students who were performing. She said one morning while she was visiting with the ringmaster, who is a special friend of hers—she calls him Roy—a woman came to apply for a job. It was Belle!"

"Was she all right?" Woodrow said quickly.

"I think so!" Mama said excitedly. "Miz Lincoln said she walked close enough to her so that she got a good look at her face, and she was sure it was Belle Prater."

"She was all right," Woodrow said, letting out a long breath. He smiled then for the first time that day. Mama returned his smile and patted his hand.

"Well, did they give her a job?" I asked.

"Yes. Miz Lincoln said they hired her on the spot, to sell popcorn and peanuts in the stands."

"So she's with the circus!" Woodrow exclaimed.

"But people from Coal Station go to the circus in Bluefield all the time," I said. "Surely somebody would've recognized her."

"Not if she's a clown!" Mama said with a big grin.

Woodrow was so tickled he laughed out loud. "My mama a clown?"

"Yes," Mama said. "All the vendors are dressed as clowns."

"Then she really is in Bluefield?" Grandpa said.

"That's what we don't know," Mama said. "Miz Lincoln said it was probably a temporary job."

"Temporary?"

"Right. When they are in a town, the circus hires local people to do things like that. The temps don't usually stay with the circus, but some have been known to join. We don't know if Belle joined or not."

"Did Miz Lincoln say anything about Joseph?" Woodrow asked.

"Yes, Joseph is adjusting to his new home and school. Everything is going well for them so far. Y'all were right about her. She's a very nice lady."

"Yeah, I need to go back next Saturday," Woodrow said. "I'll look for Mama just one more time, and I also wanna see Joseph and Miz Lincoln."

Porter popped in the back door just as Granny set a plateful of ham salad sandwiches on the table. We teased him about knowing exactly when to make an entrance. Then all hands went to the sandwiches.

"Miz Lincoln gave us her telephone number, so you can call her if you like, Woodrow," Mama said. "She has already written to her friend Roy, the ringmaster, to see if she can find out anything more."

"And where is this ringmaster now?" Grandpa said.

"With the circus in Florida for the winter."

We sat eating and absorbing this new information.

"We have news for you, too," Woodrow said after a while, and pulled the letter from Aunt Belle out of his pocket. He tossed it on the table, and Mama picked it up and began to read. Her pink mouth fell open and she gasped. When she was finished, she handed it to Granny without saying a word.

Granny read quickly, passed it on to Porter, then asked, "Where did this come from?"

So as we ate in Granny's cozy, civilized kitchen, with heat coming out of the registers at our feet, the three of us told of our adventure in Crooked Ridge.

That very afternoon, because there was an ongoing investigation and he had to inform the law, Grandpa took the letter to the sheriff, along with the information from Miz Lincoln. The sheriff took Miz Lincoln's phone number and said he would call her to get the address of the ringmaster in Florida. By Monday morning the whole town knew more'n we did. There were rumors flying ever' whichaway. Finally, when people kept pestering us, Porter wrote a short piece for the *Mountain Echo*, in which he gave only the facts as he knew them.

On Wednesday the furniture store delivered our new TV set. It was a twenty-one-inch floor model, built into a beautiful cherry cabinet. Nobody in Coal Station could boast of a finer-looking TV set than ours.

Porter and Grandpa spent the greater part of the day stringing the antenna line up to the Christmas Tower on top of the mountain. They finished just before dark, when everybody, including Cassie, gathered around this new wonder in our living room to watch something. It didn't matter what. The two channels available to us, compliments of the Christmas Tower, came in bright and clear.

We were quietly watching the NBC News with John Cameron Swayze, when we were suddenly startled by a cry from Mama.

"Oh, my stars!" she said.

All eyes went to Mama on the sofa, and she was point-ing at me. I was sitting on the floor in front of her.

"Lice!" she gasped.

Had she said *lice*?

"I saw one crawling there in the crown of your head!" Mama screeched.

"Me?" I said, placing both hands over my heart, desper-ately hoping she did not mean *my* head.

But alas, yes. That's what she meant. My face went hot with humiliation.

"I saw the creature with my own two eyes!" Mama spoke with so much outrage it was comical.

In fact, Porter, Grandpa, and Woodrow nearabout choked to death, trying not to laugh, but they were un-successful.

"You can laugh!" Mama said angrily. "But head lice are serious business. They lay their eggs down close to the scalp, and they're nearly impossible to get rid of."

"Nonsense," Granny chimed in. "I can get rid of lice in no time with my special remedy. I just need to go home and fetch my supplies. I'll be right back."

With that, Granny happily scampered out the door like a kid, seeming delighted with my violated cranium. It gave her an opportunity to show off her lice-killing talent.

While waiting for her, I imagined tiny highways and

tunnels and nests in my hair where the invaders were scampering about merrily. I resisted a powerful urge to claw at my scalp.

"I betcha a dollar she caught 'em from the Luckys," Cassie said.

"The what?" Mama said.

"The Lucky children from Lucky Ridge on the bus," Cassie went on. "Their hair is so dirty and matted up, anything could hide in there. And they were hanging all over us."

Mama let out a long weary sigh. "I can't believe it. My own daughter has caught head lice."

"The future debutante?" Woodrow said impishly. "Them varmints don't care whose head they jump onto, do they?"

"I guess not!" I snapped at him. "On the way to Crooked Ridge I noticed you about scratched a hole in your scalp!"

Woodrow's face went from mischievous to startled. "Huh? I did?"

"I've been scratching a lot, too," Cassie confessed.

Granny came back in the door, carrying various items in a box.

"Better treat all three of them," Mama said to her.

Granny did not hear her, but it was okay. She had already made that decision.

"You young'uns go to the bathroom and wet your

heads real good in warm water," she said to us, "then come back in here."

"Me too?" Woodrow said.

"Of course you too. And Cassie. Lice love to jump around from one head to another. Y'all go on now, do as I tell you."

We did as she said, and when we returned to Granny, she instructed us to sit on the floor in front of the fire-place. She had some white cloths that she spread over our laps, then she gave us fine-tooth combs, which we were to use for raking our scalps as close as we could, and see what would fall on the cloth.

We started combing, and lo and behold, little brown critters started falling from hair to cloth—and not just my hair, I was delighted to see, but Woodrow's and Cassie's, too!

"Don't let 'em get away!" Granny hollered. "You gotta catch 'em and throw 'em in the fireplace!"

We followed instructions, but I had so many lice I couldn't even catch them all, and I had to wad them up in the cloth and throw the whole thing in the fire. Then Granny gave me a fresh cloth.

After ten minutes the lice stopped falling, and we fig-ured we had them all.

"Now we gotta put this stuff on your heads," Granny said, and she brought out this stinking paste in an old battered pot. "We rub this in good all over and let it stay for a half hour. Then you can go wash it out with sham-poo."

"What for?" I said. "We got all the lice out."

"The nits are still there," Granny said calmly, "just waiting to hatch."

And she began to rub the stuff in my hair first. Morti-fied and stinking, the three of us sat there watching TV, with our hair pasted to our scalps for half an hour. All the while Mama acted like somebody had died, and Por-ter and Grandpa made wisecracks, thoroughly enjoying the show.

"I wouldn't laugh if I were you," Granny snapped at them suddenly. "You've been near these young'uns, and it wouldn't surprise me a bit to find a few lice in your heads, too. Put that in your newspaper, Mr. Re-Porter!"

At which Grandpa and Porter shut up.

19 ◀

After the lice incident, it was Porter who once again persuaded Mama to let me return to Bluefield.

"You have to let her go, Love," he said to Mama. "Yes, there are bad things in the world. There are bad people. There are poor children. There is filth, and disease, and lice. But you have to let Gypsy go to find her own way in the world. You can't protect her forever."

I thought it was a stunning speech, and it made my eyes sting a bit. I could only marvel at what a brilliant man he was.

That Saturday, on the Black and White Transit bus, Woodrow, Cassie, and I breathed a sigh of relief on reaching Lucky Ridge to discover that the Lucky children were not waiting to board the bus. This time the trip was uneventful, almost boring. When we reached Bluefield, the sky was perfectly blue, and the temperature mild. We headed straight for 111 Appalachian Street.

Joseph and Miz Lincoln, who were expecting us, came out the door with big smiles before we had a chance to knock. We greeted one another and went inside, where Miz Lincoln had soup and sandwiches ready for an early lunch. We settled around the table in her pleasant kitchen and inquired about Joseph's first two weeks with his aunt.

"Everything's good," Joseph said happily. He was wearing new clothes. His face was more relaxed than it had been the last time we saw him, and his eyes were sparkling.

"Can you walk to school?" Woodrow asked.

"No. There's a white school close to us, but blacks are bused to our own school. I've made some friends on the bus and got picked for the basketball team my first day."

"Wow! Y'all got a basketball team in the seventh grade?" Woodrow said.

"It's just competition between the grades. But we beat the eighth grade the other day. Whooped 'em good."

We didn't want to tell Miz Lincoln and Joseph about the head lice, but Mama had made us promise that we would, just in case Joseph had caught a bug or two himself. With shamed faces and apologies we gave them the disgusting news so they could be on the lookout.

Joseph said, "Oooo . . . nasty!" and went running to a mirror, as if he might detect the vermin running around in his hair.

Miz Lincoln merely laughed. "Tell your folks it takes more than a few head lice to scare me," she said. "In the circus we occasionally had infestations of everything from bedbugs and lice to ticks and fleas. We blamed it on the animals. Whatever it was, I learned all the remedies. Besides, Joseph hasn't been scratching, have you, son?"

"Not until now," Joseph said, then went into a fit of scratching, the likes of which we had never seen.

Of course he was just puttin' on, and we laughed at him.

After eating we headed out to continue our search. Joseph went with us, promising his aunt to return before dark. This time Woodrow had brought several pictures of Aunt Belle. We discussed splitting up so that we could cover more territory, but we decided against it for fear of being lost from each other. We also felt more confident together than apart. All afternoon, we trudged up and down the Bluefield streets, showing the pictures of Aunt Belle and asking about her. But once again, we had no luck at all.

On the way home, Woodrow was quiet. We were

going up the mountain toward Lucky Ridge when he turned to me and said, "I'll make one more effort. I'm gonna place an ad in the Bluefield paper. But that's it. I'm not going to Bluefield again to look for her. It's plain to me now she left for her own reasons, and she'll contact me when she's ready."

And that was that. At least we knew now that Aunt Belle was alive, and perhaps that was enough for Woodrow.

Two weeks later we had a call from Miz Lincoln in which she informed us that her letter to Roy, the ringmaster, had been returned because the circus, apparently, had moved on. There was no forwarding address.

"Sometimes they go to Mexico after the holidays," Miz Lincoln explained. "And I'm betting that's where they are."

The sheriff got the same information. And nothing new came to light.

Porter helped Woodrow place an ad in the personals of the *Bluefield Daily Telegraph*. It read: "To B.P. Please call soon I miss you From W.P."

In the same paper the sheriff placed another picture of Aunt Belle with the caption "Have You Seen This Woman?" Neither the ad nor the photo brought a response.

The days following were cold and dreary. Woodrow lapsed into moodiness again, but this time he was not hateful to me. He was quiet and patient, treating me with kindness and respect, even when he felt bad. I thought he had battled something in himself and won. Maybe my New Year's Revelation would not be necessary after all.

2 0 ◄

The next thing we knew, it was time for Grandpa and Doc Dot to take Woodrow to Baltimore for the long-awaited operation on his eyes. For several days the three of them were bustling around getting ready, packing things in suitcases, and laying out maps on Granny's kitchen table to plan their route. Doc Dot was on the phone with his friend Dr. Bridges in Baltimore almost every day. He was to operate on Woodrow's eyes. Grandpa had to take his car to get the oil changed and have the tires checked. Woodrow was trying to get ahead in his schoolwork so he wouldn't miss too much, but he was too distracted to concentrate.

And me? Well, I was watching the whole thing and feeling left out. It was silly, I know, but I wanted to go, too. I had never been to Baltimore, either.

"It's not a pleasure trip," Mama reminded me.

On the Saturday morning of their departure, I walked

out to Grandpa's car with Woodrow to stash his suitcase. Then we stood there waiting for Doc and Grandpa.

I could tell Woodrow was nervous, but I didn't know how much until he said, "If I don't make it, Gypsy—"

I interrupted him with a laugh. I know I shouldn't have, and I didn't mean to, but I did.

"Oh, Woodrow, you don't die from eye operations," I said.

He bristled. "No, but you can die from ether. Some people don't ever come out of it, you know."

"But *you* will. You know you will."

"How can you be sure?"

I shrugged. "Because you're Woodrow Prater. You always come out of everything smelling like a rose, no matter what!"

He grinned then, and said, "Well, anyhow, if I wake up dead, you can have my comic book collection."

We had daily reports from Baltimore, but I didn't see Woodrow again until Thursday afternoon, when I looked out of Granny's window and saw him being helped out of the car by Grandpa. He had his eyes all bandaged up. He was led into the house by Grandpa on one side and Doc Dot on the other.

"All went well," Doc Dot said to Granny as she hugged Woodrow to her. "Like we told you on the phone, Dr. Bridges says he believes the operation 'took.'"

"Glory be," Granny said. "So our boy's not going to be cross-eyed anymore?"

"We believe not," Doc Dot said.

Then he told us goodbye and went on home to see his wife and daughters, while Grandpa went upstairs to take a nap and Granny helped Woodrow get settled on the couch. He stretched out and sighed.

"Want some iced tea?" Granny said to him.

"That would be swell, Granny," he said, and she left the room.

"Hey there," I said to him then.

"Oh, hey, Gypsy," he said, and smiled in my direction. "I didn't know you were here."

"Did it hurt?"

"No, I didn't feel a thing till I woke up. I had a splitting headache the next night, but the nurse gave me a magic pill for it."

"You haven't looked in the mirror yet?"

"No, Doc said I have to wait another week to take the bandages off my eyes. They gotta heal good in the dark."

"Well, I collected all of your homework assignments from all of your classes. I'll help you with them later."

Woodrow groaned. "Let's save them for the weekend."

Granny brought in iced tea for both of us, then hurried back to the kitchen, where she had supper cooking on the stove.

Late that evening Woodrow, Grandpa, Granny, Dawg,

and I were listening to a radio show instead of watching television—for Woodrow's sake—when somebody knocked on the front door. Grandpa went to see who it was.

"Well, hello there, Benny!" we heard him say. "Come in, come in!"

Blind Benny was a man who had little bitty eyes he couldn't see out of, and he wandered around at night with a sack collecting stuff that people left out for him. He had a wonderful voice, and he sang while he walked up and down the streets. He lived in a room over the hardware store on Main Street, and the dogs all loved him and followed him around.

Most folks couldn't tolerate Benny because of his appearance, but Woodrow had made friends with him, and when I got to know him, I didn't mind how he looked. In all my years I had never known him to go into anybody's house, but there he was standing in Granny and Grandpa's living room. Grandpa led him to a seat and took his coat.

"I come to see the boy," Benny said. "Is he about?"

"I'm ri'cheer, Benny!" Woodrow said, smiling broadly. "I got my eyes bandaged up. Ain't we a pair, though?"

"Yeah," Benny said with a laugh. "One of us is blind, and the other'un kaint see!"

They both laughed heartily.

"How ye feelin'?" Benny said.

"Feelin' good," Woodrow said.

Dawg came up to Benny, sniffed him all over, and wagged her tail like crazy.

"Yeah, I knowed ye wuz there," Benny said to her softly, as he went rummaging around in his pocket. "And I brung ye a treat."

He brought out what looked like a piece of baloney wrapped in waxed paper and stuck it under Dawg's nose. She gobbled it up quick.

"How'd ye like that Baltymore?" Benny asked Woodrow.

"I had only one day to see it," Woodrow said. "We got there on Saturday night, checked into this hotel close to the hospital, and went out to eat fresh seafood at the waterfront. While we et two flounders apiece, we watched the boats come in.

"When we got up Sunday morning, we went sightseeing, and saw lots of interestin' stuff. But Sunday evening I had to check into the hospital so they could prep me for the surgery. That's what they call it—prepping.

"Monday morning I had the operation. It took nearabout two hours, but I didn't wake up till three o'clock. The doctor kept me Tuesday and Wednesday, and this morning he let me go. Doc Dot is going to take off the bandages for me next Wednesday. Then we'll see what we'll see."

On the designated day, as Doc Dot began to take the bandages off, I could see that Woodrow was nervous, and so was I. I reckon we all were. Around and around, the wrap was slowly unraveled.

"Like unwinding a mummy," I said, and Woodrow and I laughed uneasily.

Finally there was nothing but patches left, one on each eye.

"Don't open yet," Doc warned him as he turned off the lamp beside Woodrow's chair. "Sudden light could be painful."

Then he removed the final patches.

"Open slowly," Doc said.

And Woodrow did. He blinked several times, closed his eyes, then opened them again and looked around careful at the faces in front of him. Me and Grandpa, Granny, Mama, Porter, and Doc Dot were all there crowding in close, trying to see his eyes.

"Well, there's all them funny-lookin' people," he joked, "just like I remember 'em. So at least I know I ain't blinded."

"You got red in the whites," Granny said. "But I'll declare, I believe you got you some straight eyes."

"Nice!" Doc Dot said, with a huge grin on his face. "The blood spots will clear out in no time at all, and you are gonna have eyes as clear and blue as a Virginia sky, my boy!"

"And straight?" Woodrow said eagerly.

"Of course straight! Of course!"

"Yeah, yeah," Grandpa said, pleased as could be. "Good job. Good job."

Doc Dot then held a mirror in front of Woodrow. He looked, and his face broke into a grin. He glanced around at us and kept on grinning, gazed at his reflection again, and grinned some more.

"What you need now is a pair of attractive glasses," said Mama, the fashion expert. "And we'll go buy you some as soon as your eyes clear up."

"Then he'll have to beat the girls off with a stick," Doc Dot said as he went to the phone to report to Dr. Bridges in Baltimore.

It was the sweetest spring in anybody's memory. The apple blossoms and azaleas brightened our world with even more pink and white than in the previous spring when Woodrow had first come to us. It was hard to believe that a whole year had passed.

On a Sunday evening in April, when the breeze was sprinkling apple blossoms over the green lawn, and the frogs were croaking themselves hoarse down in Slag Creek, Woodrow's daddy, Everett, called to tell him he now had a job and a place to live in Roanoke. He invited Woodrow to come visit him and his fiancée, but he didn't say when. That prob'ly meant it wouldn't happen.

For the next two days Woodrow was very quiet, and I figured he was in the mullygrubs again, but then on the third day he perked up. For weeks we had been studying serious poetry in Mr. Collins's class. It was not Woodrow's best subject, but on that day he asked permission to recite a poem, which he said was his favorite. Mr. Collins gave him the floor. The poem went like this:

> *Old Granny Blair, what'cha doin' there?*
> *Settin' in the cotton patch, lookin' fer a bear.*
> *Bear didn't come, but a rabbit passed.*
> *Picked me up a rock and hit 'im in the ankle.*

It was a hit with the class. They laughed and repeated Woodrow's poem for the rest of the day.

As for Mr. Collins, he said simply, "Hmm . . . mm, interesting rhyme scheme."

That spring Woodrow and I spent a lot of time in the orchard, and in the wonderful tree house my father had built for me. It was our favorite place for sharing secrets and dreams. Sometimes Cassie came over to visit, and we three talked about important stuff like juvenile delinquency, segregation, and whether or not President Eisenhower was doing a good job. Cassie told us about important events from the history of our country. Woodrow often had letters from Joseph, which he shared with us. They wrote to each other about every week.

In the cool spring nights I slept with my window open so I could hear the mellow voice of Blind Benny. He often sang me to sleep.

*"In the sweet by and by,
We shall meet on that beautiful shore . . ."*

Then grade school was over. There was a graduation
ceremony the last week of May, and we, the graduating
seventh graders, stood in a receiving line all dressed up
in our formal clothes, while people shook hands with us
and treated us like adults. Next year we would be moving on to the eighth grade, which was considered the
first year of high school.

But for now, school was out, and we would not worry
about it again until the day after Labor Day. Another
golden summer lay before us with its promise of black-
berries and debutante celebrations, sunburns, birthday
dinners at Granny's house, wienie roasts, romping with
Dawg, wading in the creek, afternoon movies during
summer rains.

One Friday me and Granny and Mama had gone to the
Family Shoppe to look at their new line of sundresses,
Porter was in his office, and Grandpa was gone to the
barbershop. He had urged Woodrow to go with him and
get his hair cut, too, but Woodrow didn't want to bother
with it that day. That's how it happened that Woodrow
was all alone when the most important phone call of his
life came.

But it was not long before everybody in Coal Station

knew about it. Here came Woodrow down the street looking for us and hollerin', "Mama called me! Mama called! She's okay! She's fine! Hey, Gypsy, Mama finally called!"

He was collecting quite a crowd of people. Grandpa came out of the barbershop and found Woodrow spilling the news to me and Granny and Mama, and everybody else who happened to be on Main Street that day. Then here came Porter the Reporter, with a pad and pen, ready to tell all in the newspaper.

"We talked for a long time," Woodrow gushed. "She sounds real good. In fact, she seems happier'n a pig in slop. Grandpa, the circus is opening in Bluefield on Sunday—day after tomorrow—and Mama wants you to bring me to meet her under the big top! We can go, can't we?"

Grandpa laughed and slapped Woodrow on the back. "What do you think?"

Later at dinner Woodrow tried to recall and repeat the whole conversation between him and his mama.

"She says she was nearabout crazy when she left Crooked Ridge. Says she came to herself wandering around the streets of Johnson City, Tennessee, dressed in my clothes and shoes. She couldn't remember much of anything. Some hobos were kind to her and took her to their camp by the railroad tracks and gave her something to eat. She stayed with them for more'n a week. Then they hopped a train and went south, but Mama stayed in Johnson City.

"After the hobos left, she decided to be a girl again, and bought herself some dresses from a secondhand shop. Then she went to a church that was advertising for someone to play the piano for their services. Once they heard her play, she was hired on the spot. The minister and his wife offered her a room in the attic of the rectory, and food. That was all they could give her, but she was grateful to get it.

"So she lived in that little attic room in Johnson City all through the winter and spring. She said her mind was in turmoil the whole time. She knew she wanted to come home to me, but she could never return to Daddy and the house on Crooked Ridge. She would go crazy if she did. So she played her heart out on the piano. She never realized before how much she had missed making music. And it was a healing balm to her."

Woodrow paused and stared thoughtfully at the wall, as if he saw Aunt Belle there.

"Finally, she missed me so much she knew she had to see me. So she left Johnson City and started working her way toward home. All the time she was trying to decide what to do about Daddy. When she hit Bluefield last summer, the circus was in town, so she got a job with them selling peanuts and popcorn, and dressed like a clown, just like Miz Lincoln said.

"So she's been with the circus all this time. They went to Florida for the winter, and after the holidays they went to Mexico, like Miz Lincoln figgered. Can you imagine my mama in Mexico? She's got so much to tell me!"

Woodrow's eyes were bright with excitement.

"Wonder why she didn't call before?" I said.

"The thing she was most afraid of was that Daddy would find her and make her go back to Crooked Ridge. She's tickled to death that he's moved away and talking about getting married again. Also, she said she wanted to accomplish something. She wanted to come home triumphant. Said she wanted to *be* somebody. I don't know what she meant by that. Don't she know she always *was* somebody?"

There was a pained expression in Woodrow's new blue eyes when he said that.

"What about New Year's Eve, Woodrow?" Porter asked. "Was that her on the phone?"

"Yeah, that was her," Woodrow said. "See, Mama has found a good friend in the circus. Her name's Yvonne, and she's from Bluefield. So Mama rode up with her to spend the holidays with Yvonne's family.

"She was even thinking about coming on to Coal Station for a visit, but she chickened out. She was too skeered of running into Daddy. Still, she was dying to wish me a happy birthday, so she called. But when she heard Porter say hello, she lost her nerve. Said she froze. Then she knew she still wadn't quite ready. So she stayed quiet.

"And you know what?" he said. At this point I thought Woodrow would bust with joy. "She said she has saved up enough money for me to have my eye operation!"

We all screamed with glee.

"You didn't tell her!" Mama squealed.

"No, I didn't. I want to see the look on her face when she sees my new eyes," Woodrow said.

"Well, one thing still troubles me considerable," Granny said. "How in the world did she get out of Crooked Ridge that morning? How did she get over those steep mountains?"

Woodrow's face took on a troubled expression.

"That's the part I don't understand, either," he said softly. "The explanation she gave . . . Well, it sounds crazy. She said she came to herself in Johnson City, and she couldn't remember how she got there, but she said . . . she thought . . . she believes . . ."

He stumbled and stopped.

"What? What?" We all wanted to know.

"She flew," Woodrow said.

2 2 ◀

When the circus opened in Bluefield that Sunday afternoon in June, a whole bunch of us were in a special section that had been reserved for us under the big top. I sat with Woodrow, Cassie, Joseph, and Doc Dotson's twins, DeeDee and Dottie. Right behind us were Mama and Porter, Granny and Grandpa, Pap Caulborne, Mr. Collins, Miz Lincoln, Doc Dot, and Irene. All around us was about half the population of Coal Station, all there not just to see the circus but also hoping to catch a glimpse of Belle Prater.

Aunt Belle had told Woodrow that he was to stay put on the first row, and she would find him, but he was having a hard time sitting still. He kept looking around, behind, in front, to either side. There were clowns in the stands selling popcorn and peanuts, cigarettes and candy and pop, even cotton candy, but we couldn't identify

Aunt Belle as being one of them. They were all too short or too tall or too fat, or they were obviously men.

Then it was time for the show to start, and the ringmaster stood before us with a microphone in his hand.

"That's my friend Roy," Miz Lincoln whispered loudly.

"Ladies and gentlemen!" Roy bellowed to the crowd. "Today for our opening act we have a once-in-a-lifetime show for you. Let your eyes follow the lights!"

The lights fell to the center of the circus tent, where we saw a raised platform serving as a stage. At the rear of the stage was a dark curtain, and standing in front of the curtain was a short, chubby man with a handlebar mustache and a goatee. He was dressed in a black tuxedo, complete with cape, top hat, and cane. In the spotlight he smiled broadly at the eager audience and spread his arms wide. The cape opened, revealing a shiny royal blue lining.

"Presenting the most unusual magic show on earth!" continued the ringmaster. "Blundering Bill!"

The magician walked to the front edge of the stage. He started to bow and tip his hat to the crowd, but his exaggerated bow toppled him over the edge of the stage, where he sprawled in a pile of sawdust. His top hat went flipping through the air until it landed on the head of a clown, who just "happened" to be walking by. The hat fell down over the clown's eyes, and he took off running, bumping into things, falling and bouncing to his feet again, yelling, "I'm blind! I'm blind!"

When the laughter had died down, Blundering Bill sheepishly walked back up the steps to the stage, brushing sawdust from his snappy clothes as he went. When he had almost regained his composure, he slipped on a banana peel and his feet went flying all over again. Thus began a magic show that made us laugh so hard we almost forgot why we were there.

Instead of pulling rabbits out of a hat, Blundering Bill pulled mice out of his hair. Instead of pulling a long string of scarves from his sleeve, Blundering Bill pulled a long string of slimy boogers from his nose. Instead of plucking coins from his ears, Blundering Bill pulled a string of sausages right through his head, in one ear and out the other.

All this time we could hear the circus pianist playing a catchy popular tune called "Cherry Pink and Apple-Blossom White."

Blundering Bill fell off the stage for the last time, and the spotlight left him to go back to the ringmaster.

"And now, ladies and gentlemen, I am sure the fine piano playing that accompanied Blundering Bill's act has not escaped your notice. Please allow me to introduce the lovely and lively BluBelle!"

With these words the spotlight left the ringmaster and

fell once again on the stage, where the curtain had been lifted to reveal a petite woman sitting at a piano. All her concentration was on the keyboard in front of her. As the light made sparklers on her glittery blue dress, she began to play "The Bluebells of Scotland." At the same time the clowns held up cue cards on which were printed the words to the song in large letters. The audience began to sing along:

> "Oh where, tell me where is your highland laddie gone?
> Oh where, tell me where is your highland laddie gone?
> He's gone with streaming banners where noble deeds are
>   done.
> And it's oh! in my heart I wish him safe at home.
>
> "Oh where, tell me where did your highland laddie dwell?
> Oh where, tell me where did your highland laddie dwell?
> He dwelt in bonnie Scotland where bloom the sweet
>   bluebells
> And it's oh! in my heart I rue the laddie well."

"They sing like this after each act," Miz Lincoln was whispering to us. "It gives the next act a chance to set up."

At that moment the woman at the piano finished the last verse of the song. Then she turned to her audience, smiled, and began to blow kisses to us. And yes, it was a familiar face we saw. A gasp went up from our section of the bleachers, and Woodrow was on his feet immediately. But he did not call to her as I expected. He simply stood there grinning and staring at the figure he had missed so desperately for all these months.

We had to wait until the show was over to see Aunt Belle and talk to her up close, but we had been waiting for a long time, so what was another hour? Finally, she left the stage and walked straight to Woodrow and gathered him to her heart. With her face flushed with excitement, she seemed transformed, almost beautiful. Her gown was the same color as her eyes, which were as bright and blue as Woodrow's.